Chapter One
A Mundane Life

High School—ugh. It seemed as though the popular crowd enjoyed it, probably because of the unlimited social interactions it provided them. But for me it was nothing more than a giant cesspool of snobby, self-centered, browbeating parasites. The social divisions never changed. It always puzzled me how the most popular, privileged brats got to decide how everyone else was to be treated. What joy it would bring to my soul to see the socialites squirm on the bus ride to school, not knowing what torment awaited them. Instead, I was the one encased in that yellow casket, being delivered by its balding, overweight driver, to the vultures in the schoolyard.

While the bus made its rounds, picking up the school's victims, I couldn't help but notice the look of despair we all shared. Every face wore the same anxious look, up to the final stop. The last one to climb aboard the chariot of torture was Kevin, who had been my best friend since kindergarten. In fact, as I thought about it, he had been my only friend since kindergarten. He was a tall kid with pale skin, shaggy hair, and a love for black clothing. Besides the obvious reasons that made him a target, he had the ultimate curse: his last name was McCool. The countless hours of torture he endured by the browbeaters for his last name alone would rival those of the rest of the passengers combined. Still, he never allowed the bullying to bother him. He always wore a bright smile on his face and was constantly preoccupied by his obsession with horror folklore, role-playing games, and the string of killings by wild beasts making news in the state. I found his logic behind it unhinged, and I hoped he didn't bring it up this morning.

As Kevin made his way to the rear of the bus, I couldn't help but feel sorry for myself. I was fifteen and handsome enough. My sandy-blond hair, blue eyes, big smile, and trendy clothes should have scored me a place with the more popular crowd. Yet I was still exiled to dwell amongst the castaways. I often wondered if it was my association with Kevin that kept me out of the in-crowd; however, betrayal of our friendship was never an option. He had always been there for me, and, even then, I knew a friend of that magnitude came around once in a lifetime. All the superficial acquaintances in the world wouldn't justify throwing that out the window, even if it meant I would no longer be on the receiving end of the browbeaters' hostility.

"Chamberlain High School, here we come." Kevin plunked down into the seat next to me and dropped his backpack on the floor.

"Oh boy," I said, "a new school year, same old agony."

"Come on, Connell. It's going to be different this year. We're not the freshmen."

Kevin sounded so confident I almost wanted to believe him, but I knew better. The last time I bought into that crap was our final year of middle school. Eighth grade was supposed to be our break-

2

out year, the year where it was our turn to rule. Instead, we found ourselves at the beck and call of sixth and seventh graders who were considered cool enough to hang out with the popular eighth graders. In fact, it got so bad that year that Kevin once had his head dunked into a toilet for their amusement.

"You've said that every first day of school since the fourth grade, but nothing changes. The popular kids rule the school, and we're the doormats. When are you going to wake up and face reality? I know I don't have to remind you about eighth grade, do I?"

"It's just a gut feeling." He leaned back and put his knees up on the back of the seat in front of him. "This year is going to be different. I can't put my finger on it, but something enormous is going to occur for the both of us."

"Well, I'll believe that when I see it," I said.

"Hey, that reminds me, can you believe there was another attack last night," he said, pulling out his journal of newspaper clippings.

"Kevin, how many times do we have to go over this? They're either wild dogs or some crazy cult of sick individuals," I reminded him, pushing the clippings away from my face.

Slamming the journal on his lap he sighed and said, "Why are you so closed-minded? Can't you see the pattern? They only attack during full moons."

"So what? My dad used to tell me that Mom acted crazy every full moon—does that mean she went around murdering people?"

Rolling his eyes and turning the page, Kevin responded, "Why do you always go there? I think you joke about it to cover up how much that situation still haunts you."

Looking out the window I noticed the school parking lot on the horizon and sighed. "At least their deaths were because of a car crash and not part of some crazy theory you cooked up in your head."

"It's not crazy—you'll see one day and it will not be pretty," he snapped back.

I laughed out loud and shot back, "I think I have a better chance of my parents coming back to life first and walking on water."

The bus pulled into Chamberlain's parking lot. I could see the famous Chief's Head where all the outcasts met to avoid the vermin of this despicable place. For the school and its collection of aristocrats, it shined green at night after every athletic victory. Though, for us oddballs, it was a safe haven during school hours. The popular kids wouldn't dare to step foot around the Chief's Head during the day. The threat of being linked with our group overshadowed any desire to terrorize one of us.

Approaching the drop-off point, the bus driver slowed down to a crawl. He would always say it was because of traffic, but I didn't believe him. It seemed he got pleasure out of seeing the intimidation on his passengers' faces as we passed by the swarm of popular kids. This driver wanted to make sure that they got a good look at their prey, and, like a pride of lions, they were deciding which gazelle they would set their sights on for the day. I always had the feeling that the driver did this so he would be deemed worthy of the pride. I thought it likely he once was in our shoes and was still looking to break out of our group. A chill went down my spine with the thought of this label continuing beyond high school. However, I prayed it was nothing more than his desire to fit in with their crowd that made him linger for acceptance. My plans were to flee as far as I could after graduation and never look back.

Like a herd of sheep, we all piled off the bus and headed straight to the Chief's Head. Most of the group did their best to avoid eye contact as the crowd of bullies began to approach us. Like always, Kevin brought up the rear of the pack. I couldn't bring myself to leave him alone, so I stopped, knowing that I'd just sacrificed my own safety.

"Will you come on," I shouted, waving my arms hysterically.

"Calm down. I told you, we aren't the freshmen anymore, we have nothing to worry about," Kevin reasoned as he caught up to me.

However, it was too late. We were separated from the herd and, just like that, we were surrounded.

"Hey, McCool, it's your lucky day. I have decided that you're going to be my personal do boy this year," Jack Alexander proclaimed.

Jack was a junior this year and the star quarterback of the football team. He had always been a dirt bag, and as his status grew in the pride of the popular, so had his arrogance. But the fact that he started bullying Kevin even before the first bell of the first day amazed me.

"Jack, I think you have things mixed up. You see, we aren't freshmen anymore, so the group of kids you're searching for are already under the head," Kevin argued reasonably.

"McCool, you have to be the biggest idiot I've ever met. I don't care that you're a sophomore. What I do care about is my homework being done every day and handed over to me by seven o'clock the next morning. Do you get me?" Jack head-butted Kevin with his huge forehead. I could see blood splatter from Kevin's nose as he gasped in pain.

"Why don't you leave him alone," I shouted, pushing Jack away.

Before I realized what I'd done, Jack's henchmen grabbed a hold of me and held me tight. I knew I was about to receive my first beating of the year and I couldn't help but think how wrong Kevin was. While it was a new grade, it was the same school with the same crap.

"You must think you're a big man, Connell. Well, I'm about to teach you your first lesson of the year." Jack squared up and punched me in the stomach with all his might.

I dropped to my knees in agony as his cronies let go of me. The thought of enduring three more years of this punishment raced through my mind as I gasped for breath.

"Connell, are you okay?" Kevin asked, kneeling down beside me clutching his nose.

"I'm not done speaking to you, McCool," Jack said as he grabbed a hold of Kevin's hair and pulled him up. "My homework, McCool, what time are you going to have it to me?"

Kevin looked at the ground. "Seven o'clock, every morning." Blood was smeared across his face.

"Good boy, McCool, I'll see you later," he said, smacking Kevin in the head a few times for fun.

Kevin helped me to my feet as Jack and his pals walked away, laughing. The pain was subsiding and I could see how devastated Kevin was, so I decided not to lay into him for his stupidity.

"Thanks for sticking up for me, Connell," he said, taking a water bottle out of his bag. He cleaned the blood off his face.

"Don't worry about it, that's what friends do for each other. Now, let's get out of here before he decides to come back."

For the rest of the morning, Kevin and I kept a low profile. We dashed from room to room to avoided Jack Alexander at all costs. It became clear to me that our luck had shifted for the better since our altercation this morning. We had been to about half our classes, and none of the pukes from the parking lot were in any of them. Instead, the classes were made up of a perfect combination of outcasts and normal kids who were able to sail under the browbeaters' radar. At that point, I would even have taken that status over the one my friendship with Kevin placed me in, but I knew it wouldn't help. Even if I'd decided to drop Kevin altogether, my altercation with Jack placed me in the sights of the football team as well as anyone else Jack appointed for the rest of the year.

When the bell rang at the end of math class, all I could do was sigh. The loud siren was the signal to Jack and his followers to begin their hunt of the outcasts in the cafeteria. I had always chosen the safe route of packing my lunch every day. It allowed me to bypass the torture chamber altogether and go straight to the Chief's Head. Kevin, on the other hand, for whatever reason, refused to take my advice. Instead he would always risk humiliation or bodily damage for two slices of pizza from our cafeteria. Usually he came out of lunchroom with at least one slice down his pants, or in his hair, or worse. However, Kevin, being Kevin, never allowed it to get the best of him, and that was what I admired the most about him. He had a mental toughness that was out of the ordinary for an outcast. I think most of the kids in our group would wet their pants at the very thought of going into the cafeteria versus actually doing it every day.

Eating my sandwich and chips, I envisioned where the slice of pizza would be today, yet, to my amazement, he came around the corner with both slices on his tray. Not only was the pizza on his tray, he was also carrying the tray of a freshman he was talking with. She was a petite girl with short, dark hair, brown eyes, and dimples. What stood out to me the most was her clothing. She was dressed in army fatigues, combat boots, and she had dog tags around her neck. I have to admit, while the outfit was not impressive at all, she was cute and seemed to have a bubbly personality.

"Hey, Connell, I want you to meet Lilly," Kevin said while they took a seat on the bench next to me.

I didn't respond at first; all I could do was stare at them with my mouth wide open, which I assumed exposed a chewed-up piece of my sandwich. After all, what was Kevin doing with a girl, even if she did look like a soldier?

"Earth to Connell, you there, buddy?" he said, waving his hand in front of my face.

"Sorry … hey, I'm Connell, and—what was your name again?"

"I'm Lilly, Kevin has told me so much about you," she said, chuckling softly.

"Exactly when did you meet?" I asked, still in denial.

"Over the summer. Lilly works at Horror and Things, in Ybor City," Kevin told me before biting into his pizza.

"Horror and Things … what kind of place is that?"

"Well … we supply all the tools, literature and weapons needed to kill monsters," she answered as if I should have known.

"Uh, huh … So you believe in that nonsense as well?"

Kevin, apparently seeing that I had offended her, jumped into the conversation. "Show her your birthmark, Connell."

"What … you told her about that?" I grumbled through my teeth.

"Sure … that was my whole reason for going to the store in the first place. They had a book about a mark of that sort."

"Mark of that sort—so you told her that you thought I was a werewolf?" I asked, placing my hand on my forehead and rubbing it in disbelief.

"Connell, how many times do I have to go over this with you? A werewolf is someone who is bitten, mutates with the full moon, and loses all self-control. You are a wolf man, someone who has the aptitude to change on a whim, yet retain their mental capacity."

"Wolf man, werewolf, who cares … it's all the same to me, and you're crazy."

"Are you going to show it to me or what?" Lilly said, interrupting us.

"Sure … I'd hate to disappoint," I snapped back.

As I rolled up my left sleeve, my anger grew at the thought of Kevin running around town telling people this crap. How was I ever going to improve my life if people continued to associate me with some kid who believes in wolf men and claims I'm one of them? I extended my arm for her to see. My birthmark had always been a source of embarrassment for me, so I constantly wore a shirt with sleeves to cover it up. After all, having a mark that resembled a five-pointed star wasn't the most crowd friendly thing to display. It was also another reason why I felt destined to be an exile for the rest of my life. Most parents thought I was some kind of devil worshiper, and, as soon as they saw it, their child was no longer allowed to talk to me. Before they died, my parents tried to get it removed, but the doctors could never get rid of it. If they cut it away with a laser, after a few weeks, I'd wake up and find it had returned. I didn't know what I'd done to warrant this curse, but I loathed it with all my being. My grandmother, who I have lived with for a while now, always tried to tell me it was a blessing in disguise, and, in time, I would understand its meaning. She always tried to make me feel better about myself and looked for the good in every situation.

"That's simply amazing," she said, scanning over it.

"What's so amazing about having a pentagram for a birthmark?" I asked in disbelief.

"I'll tell you what, if you come by the store after school, my sister and I will show you."

"Sister … does your entire family believe in this nonsense?" I sneakily responded.

Lilly laughed at me. "I would watch what you say when you get to the store. My sister will not show the same amount of patience I have towards your ignorance."

"So noted. We'll head right over after school," Kevin confirmed before I could respond.

"Great. I'll see y'all at the shop. Bye, guys, it's been real."

She stood up, picked up her tray, winked at Kevin, and walked away. We both followed her with our eyes. Kevin out of fascination, no doubt, but for me, it was more out of skepticism. Why was this girl so captivated by my birthmark? Was there an unseen agenda? Did Jack Alexander put her up to this? It was enough to spike my curiosity, which was the only reason I agreed to go along with this crusade of stupidity.

"She's amazing," Kevin said, turning back to his tray to continue to eat.

I shoved him in frustration and asked, "What's wrong with you? Why in the world would you be out there telling people that idiotic theory about me?"

"Connell, I went into their store and asked for a book. When I did, she started asking me all kinds of questions. I know how you feel about that mark and I would never do that to you."

I leaned back against the wall and sighed as I unrolled my sleeve. "Sorry, man, I just hate it so much. It's brought me nothing but heartache since I was little, and I've worked so hard to hide it."

"I know, buddy, and that's why I wouldn't do such a thing. Now, let's get going before we're late to class."

"Cool. So are we going to jump on the bus to Ybor right after school?" I asked.

"Yep, meet me back here after school, and we'll head out. I think you're going to love the shop. Besides, her older sister has to be the most beautiful girl I've ever seen. So at the bare minimum, at least you get to meet her."

"Yeah … but how old is she? Twenty? Twenty-five?"

"No, she's seventeen. She dropped out of school a few years back to run the shop," Kevin told me while we dumped our trash.

I had to admit, my interest in going to Horror and Things had just increased tenfold. If I could actually use this thing to entice a beautiful girl, I invited the opportunity. I only hoped that, unlike Lilly and Kevin, she could be reasonable and drop this nonsense.

Chapter Two
Horror and Things

The rest of the school day proceeded like a sloth making its way across a tree branch. By the last period of the day, I could have sworn the custodial staff removed the batteries from the clocks on the walls in an effort to maximize my mental anguish. After each tick of the clock, my antsy mood must have become more apparent to everyone around me. While I pondered on what awaited me at Horror and Things, I had no interest in the excessive amount of rules that Mr. Farley was going over. Mr. Farley was the economics teacher and a jerk to anyone who didn't live up to his expectations. Sometimes I thought he didn't have a life outside of the classroom. Instead of going home like a normal person, I imagined him sitting at his desk all night, deliberating on new ways to torment us with his mindless babble about how the country was in the toilet because of our generation.

After about thirty minutes of listening to his maddening voice and his absurd rules, I did the only thing that would break up his monologue. I asked to go to the bathroom, knowing it would result in a tirade of insults being hurled my way.

"Well, well, Mr. Maxwell, I'm so sorry that what I have to say isn't important enough for you to wait to use the restroom. Now I have to stop talking about what these children need to know to be successful in my class, to write you out a hall pass. Just because you

14

are determined to be a loser doesn't give you the right to take away from the valuable education that these other students deserve, now does it?"

"Mr. Farley, not to be disrespectful, but aren't you wasting more time by talking about having to stop talking, versus just writing the hall pass?" I asked in a condescending tone.

His face turned as red as the fire extinguisher hanging on the wall. I looked around at the class and saw that they all were anticipating his answer and he didn't disappoint a soul.

"Mr. Maxwell, that just cost you your Saturday. You report to school at nine o'clock for detention. Now, get up and get yourself to the office, before I decide to remove you myself. You mark my words, son, you aren't going to amount to squat in life. You will be a blood-sucking tick, living off the hard-working people of this world. There will be no give, only take from the likes of you. If this were a good thirty years ago, I would handle you myself—a good paddling would straighten you out. I can only imagine how heartbroken your grandmother would be if she was healthy enough to understand she was living with nothing more than a bum of a grandson."

Smiling, I stood up and made my way to the front of the class while Mr. Farley aggressively filled out the detention form. He slung the form at me after signing the bottom. It hit me in the chest and fell to the floor before I could catch it. I bent over, picked up the slip and gave Kevin a quick nod. He knew exactly what was coming next. I stood up, smiled at Mr. Farley, and gave him a thumbs up with the form next to my face. I immediately headed out the door, free from the last twenty minutes of his gibberish. Besides, I knew that last act on my part had Mr. Farley's blood pressure skyrocketing, aware that he didn't get the best of me. Under normal circumstances he would have the average sophomore in tears, but today, I beat him at his own game by keeping my emotions in check. It felt good.

While I made my way down to the office, I couldn't help but wonder how I managed to get him two years in a row. My guess was that he'd had such a joyful time belittling me last year that he manipulated my guidance counselor into assigning me to him again. Oh well, I'd have all semester to worry about my grades and abuse at the hands of Mr. Farley. Right now, I just wanted to turn this form in and head out of prison for the day.

Entering the main office, I gave my slip to the school vice principal, Mrs. Perry, and received the same disappointed look she gave everyone who got detention. She was new to the school this year, and from what I'd heard, she came from a school system on the east coast of the state. Kevin told anyone who would listen that he'd heard she'd seen someone killed by a wild beast, and that was what made her move. She was a little secretive and skittish, but unlike Kevin, I thought that was just her personality, and not because of some deep dark secret from the past. As she entered my name into the log, I couldn't help but notice that Jack Alexander was also on the list. I felt the smile quickly drain from my face, leaving disbelief in its wake.

16

Closing her log book she looked up at me and said, "You're all set, Mr. Maxwell."

"Thanks, Mrs. Perry."

The dismissal bell sounded, startling her, as I was about to leave the office.

"You okay, Mrs. Perry?" I asked.

Wiping her face with a dark-stained cloth from her purse, she said, "Yes, just a little jumpy, I guess."

"Okay, well, I'll see you later," I said, leaving the office.

I hustled over to meet Kevin under the Chief's Head. He walked up, shaking his head and laughing.

"Dude, you really outdid yourself with Farley today. He was so upset, he had to excuse himself twice to take some of his heartburn medicine. The second time he came back to class with a towel on his head."

"I wish I could've been there to see it. I just couldn't take sitting there anymore. His lists of rules are longer than the United States Constitution. However, the crappy news is that Jack Alexander is going to be in detention with me. Man, I can't catch a break when it comes to him." I kicked the garbage can over in frustration, thinking about how much I'd just screwed myself.

"It could be worse, Connell. Mr. Farley could be the one in charge this weekend, but instead Mrs. Perry has it."

"How do you know that?"

"In one of Farley's rants he was going on and on about how lucky you were it was Mrs. Perry's turn. Hey, don't worry about that right now. Come on, we have to catch the bus."

I broke into a sprint with Kevin across the school parking lot. After all, we were heading into enemy territory and we wanted to get to the city bus stop unscathed from Jack and his fellow maggots. While weaving in and out of cars, my smile found its way back. I realized I was now up two points on Farley. I knew that he was going to come at me with everything he had for the rest of the year; however, for now, I was going to savor today's results. As far as Jack was concerned, well, I decided that I would just deal with that on Saturday.

Reaching the bus stop without an altercation was another small victory for me. Climbing aboard the bus, I looked out the window and watched as the outcasts sprinted from the Chief's Head to the school bus. Our poor excuse of a bus driver didn't open the door immediately for them. Instead, he gave Jack and his cronies enough time to humiliate the kids at the rear of the line. After Jack slapped around a handful of them, the bus driver opened the doors. I could envision the grin on his face as he watched the terrorized victims board his yellow chariot of doom.

"One day, Kevin, they're all going to get what's coming to them," I said as we both slipped into our seats.

With the bus merging into traffic, Kevin said, "I just hope we're there to see it."

With the school day firmly behind me, my attention turned to Horror and Things. I could feel knots beginning to form in my stomach imagining what Lilly's sister looked like. This could be the big break I'd been waiting for, or it could turn out to be another disaster that Kevin suckered me into. Either way, I thought, I'd find out what to expect when we arrived.

"Okay, so give me the rundown of this place. I don't want to look like an idiot when we get there."

"Well, it's off Seventh Avenue in Centro Ybor. It looks rundown from the outside— cracked windows, chipped paint, and a faded sign. Inside is exactly what you think of in a horror flick. It's dirty, cobwebs everywhere, and the floor creaks with every step. They always have the items you typically need to combat monsters, like silver bullets, stakes, wolf's bane, spell books, and other monster repellents."

"Okay … Why in the world were you in this place? More importantly, why in the world am I going to this place?"

"Connell, don't judge it until you see it. It's really a cool place, and they have insightful material on your birthmark. Besides, I thought you wanted to see Lilly's sister."

I didn't answer him. After his description of Horror and Things, my hope that Lilly's sister wasn't as cracked as Lilly and Kevin was simply nonexistent at this point. All I wanted to do now was to get there, appease Kevin, and get out without anyone seeing me. I knew better than to agree to this, but I let my imagination run away from me. I was stuck like a chicken in a cage on its way to the slaughterhouse.

The bus finally arrived at Seventh Avenue in Centro Ybor. Kevin got up and pressed the bell, signaling to the driver that we were ready to get off. I hesitantly got up and followed him to the doors. I could tell that Kevin's eagerness was peaking, mainly because he was rambling on about my birthmark. I nodded my head and smiled every few sentences, but inside, I was sick to my stomach about my poor decision. When we got off the bus, we began the short walk up Seventh, heading towards Horror and Things. Kevin continued his mindless sermon the entire way there. I, on the other hand, kept my head down with my hands in my pockets. When we arrived at the shop, I opened the door and rushed inside with Kevin following closely behind me.

After closing the door, I took a look around and it was exactly how he'd described it—dirty, old, and eerie. The cobwebs were as thick as blankets, and there had to be at least an inch of dust on the shelves. The only thing that shined in this place was the silver that was all over the store. We made our way up to the counter, which looked abandoned, to find Lilly standing behind it.

"You made it." She ran around the counter and gave Kevin a hug.

"Wouldn't miss it for the world," he replied, smiling from ear to ear.

"Hey, Connell, how are you?" she asked politely.

"I'm good, Lilly," I lied.

"Well, make yourself at home, and I'll go and get my sister."

She disappeared to the rear of the store in a hurry. I continued to look around as I followed Kevin over to the counter. We took a seat on some stools that were fairly clean compared to the rest of the store. While we waited for Lilly to return, I couldn't help but notice all the weapons behind the counter on hooks. There were daggers, shotguns, crossbows, and handguns. This made me slightly uneasy, and when I turned to tell Kevin we needed to get to out of there, I saw her for the first time. She was tall and had long blonde hair with pink highlights. Her brown eyes were hypnotizing, and her smile was stunning. I could tell she was a southern girl based on her cowboy boots, jeans, and Alabama shirt. It was like night and day when you compared her to her sister, Lilly. While she approached, I forgot about all my concerns, and only hoped she was at least half as intrigued by me as I was by her.

"Connell, I would like you to meet my sister, Andie Rae," Lilly said.

"Hey," I said, still in a trance.

"So, you're the one who thinks we're all crazy?" she said sternly.

"Crazy … uh … I don't actually remember using the word *crazy*. Why would I say that? I mean, look at this place, it has to be the coolest place in the world." I fumbled every word.

"Uh huh," she said, before moving on to Kevin to say hello.

It started to look like game over before I had a chance to make my first move. It was clear that Lilly had told her all I had said under the Chief's Head that morning. If there was ever a day I wanted to go back and do some things over, this was it. One way or another, my birthmark continued to plague me with moments of frustration.

"So, how about you roll that sleeve up and show me what you got." She teased me with a smile.

"Yeah, sure … that's what we are here for, right?" I asked, continuing to fumble my words.

She rolled her eyes as I extended my left arm onto the counter. After she leaned in to get a closer look, she turned to the shelves behind her, pulled out a large dusty book, and placed it on the counter.

"Red Moon, White Moon," Kevin said, reading the title.

"What's that book about?" I asked.

"It reveals the origins of the wolf man and the prophecies of the annihilation of the werewolf," Lilly answered.

"So, we're going to use a book of fiction to determine what my birthmark is about. Wonderful," I said sarcastically.

"There's nothing fictitious about this book, darling. If you don't want to take this seriously, then you can get off my stool and get out of here before I throw you out," Andie Rae growled.

"Look, I'm sorry. I just have a hard time believing in this … stuff. I apologize. I do want to hear what you have to say."

I knew I was toast. I'd ruined any chance I had with this girl. But at the same time, I couldn't help feeling relieved because I now knew she was as flaky as the other two. She flipped through several pages of this massive novel and came to a picture that was identical to my birthmark.

"Here we go," she said, while the rest of us leaned in to see what she was talking about.

"You have the mark of the wolf man," Kevin read. "I told you I was right."

"Right about what, Kevin, really? This tells us nothing, it proves nothing and it is nothing," I said in disbelief.

"How about I share the details before you continue to make an idiot of yourself?" Andie Rae asked.

"Sure—at this point, I'm up for anything. I mean, the only thing I've enjoyed about this trip is seeing something as beautiful as you talk to me, but from what I gather, this conversation is leading any hopes of that going anywhere right down the tubes," I blurted out in response.

There was an awkward silence for a moment, as the three of them just stared at me. I couldn't believe what I'd just said either, but what did I have to lose? After all, this chat would be over in another five minutes or so, and then I would be heading home on a bus, returning to my boring life.

Before Andie Rae could say anything else, the front door opened and four guys came walking in.

"Girls, we found out where it's going to be. We have to get ready now, because we only have a few hours till dark," said the smallest guy in the group.

"Slow down, Toby," Lilly said. "We have guests."

"This is the one Kevin has been telling us about, the one with the mark," Andie Rae added.

I peered over at Kevin, who just shrugged his shoulders in return. As I looked back over at the four of them, I heard the front door lock. The sound sent chills down my spine. I knew I was now stuck in this madhouse, and the inmates were the ones calling the shots. Three of the four guys made their way over to the counter; the fourth opened a cooler and grabbed a cold soda. He took a seat on the end of the bar, ignoring us altogether, and began to swig down his drink. He was difficult to look at without wanting to hurl. His hair was jet black and unkempt, his arms were covered in scars from what appeared to be animal bites, and his left eye was discolored as if it had been gouged at some point.

"Connell, I'd like you to meet Toby, Doc, Bear, and that unsociable one in the corner is Hayden," Lilly said.

I nodded and waved as I scrutinized them. Toby was a young kid with thick glasses and a ton of silver spheres strapped to his clothes. Doc looked like he was a few years older than Andie Rae and carried with him what appeared to be medical supplies. Bear, well, he looked like he'd eaten a bear and lived to tell the tale. He was a massive guy, wearing a white shirt with holes in it, coveralls, and a camouflaged baseball cap.

"So this is the one, the savior?" Toby asked, examining me through his thick goggles.

"Savior … what are you talking about?" I asked.

"I reckon they done not told you all the details, yet?" Bear asked me.

"No, Bear, I was about to, but you four popped in before I had the chance," Andie Rae said. "Do you still want to hear about it?" she asked me with a firm look.

"Sure … what do I have to lose?" I asked, throwing my hands in the air.

"Okay, but no smart comments, or so help me, I will put you straight on your butt," she threatened.

"I promise. At this point, after meeting all of you, I'm curious to hear this."

"Okay—here goes. Roughly six thousand years ago, there was a boy named Kane who murdered his family. This boy was marked by a group called the Elders for life because of this terrible deed. However, Kane feared that people would take revenge on him, so one boy who still believed in redemption vowed to protect him. This boy, who was Kane's best friend prior to this terrible act, saw the good in him and believed that he'd only lost his way. Most left Kane alone out of fear, as they knew that Kane's best friend was one of the Elders' sacred wolf men. He had the ability to change into a creature that was so powerful, so lethal, that death was certain for all those who faced him. Yet, some still tried to plot against Kane, only to face their demise. As time went on, Kane became envious of the power his friend had and craved it for himself. So one night, as Kane prepared their food, he drugged the boy and restrained him. When the boy awoke, he found that Kane had extracted some of his blood and had drunk it. This boy's blood gave Kane the power he craved, but Kane used it for evil. Determined to raise an army, he would bite his victims but not kill them. The venom from Kane's fangs would be infused into their DNA, causing them to become his servants and, on every full moon, turning into mindless monsters that destroyed everything in their path. The werewolf, as Kane called them, was born, and he used his army to wipe out the Elders and their sacred wolf men. Only the boy survived the attack and was given one last charge. As they died, the Elders promised the boy another of his kind would arise and save the world from Kane and his army. They also told the boy that the moon would turn red whenever a werewolf was created, as a reminder to him of what happened that day."

"You, my friend, have the mark of the wolf man, and we think you're the one they promised would appear," Toby said, grabbing my arm and pointing to my birthmark.

I did the first thing that came to mind: I began to laugh. I knew it was a mistake as soon as I did it, but I couldn't hold it in any longer. I noticed Kevin swinging around in his stool and putting his head down. The others backed away from me slowly, and I locked eyes with Hayden, who was now walking towards me. He took one last swig of his soda and threw down the empty bottle, shattering it into pieces.

"Something funny to you?" he asked, seizing me by the shirt.

"Hey, man, I didn't mean to offend you … I just thought it was a joke, that's all," I replied quickly.

"You're the only one I see laughing, pansy, and I don't find it amusing."

"Look, I'm sorry, okay … but this is just too much for me to believe."

"Okay, pansy, so it's too much for you to believe. I tell you what, how about you and your friend come with us tonight, and we'll see what we can do to cure you of your disbelief."

"Hayden … you can't ask them to go—"

"Shut up, Lilly. They're going and that is final. This birthmark proves nothing to me. All I see is a pansy in front of me, not a savior."

He let me go and my body slammed to the ground. Hayden headed off to the back room without saying another word. Kevin didn't turn around or offer any advice on how to get us out of this mess. I wanted to kill him for getting us involved with these nut jobs. However, for now, I needed to figure out a way for us to escape.

"I reckon we need to get ready. Don't worry, boys, y'all be okay if you stay close to Hayden and me," Bear told both of us.

All I could do was smile and acknowledge that I heard him. Kevin headed off with Lilly to get ready to go; I just sat on the bench watching these maniacs load up their trench coats with weapons and a bunch of other stuff. Doc tossed me a coat to put on. As I slipped it on, I quickly prayed that wherever we were going, Kevin and I would get out alive.

Chapter Three
Charitable Feast

For the next couple of hours, I sat alone at the bar of Horror and Things, watching everyone get ready for the evening's event. All of them, including Kevin, were loading up on weapons, wolf's bane, and the silver spheres. I was offered numerous items by Toby; I refused everything he tried to give me. This was where I had to draw the line—if Kevin was stupid enough to get involved with whatever they were arming themselves for, that was his choice. After all, how many groups of kids on a Friday night put on long trench coats and pile weapons into them? None, unless they were absolutely out of their minds, and that, I was not. Yet the one person who did pique my interest was Hayden. While he did put on a coat, he didn't take any weapons. He was either a coward and would allow everyone else to do the fighting, or else he was crazy enough to charge into a situation that everyone else thought called for a weapon, without one. Based on what I knew about him, I went with the latter.

It was about six thirty at night, and they all huddled for a prayer. Well, everyone did except Hayden; he continued to stare at me from his stool at the end of the bar. I felt like he knew what I was thinking; a dash for the door while they prayed was tempting. With his piercing glare cutting through me, I decided it was in my best interest to just go with the group and see what happened. When they finished their prayer, they stood up, and Bear nodded at us. Hayden rose from the stool at the end of the bar and headed towards the front door. Bear signaled for me to follow him, and I did exactly as I was told.

"I reckon you should stay within a chew's spit of me. That's if you want to survive because we fixin' to get ourselves in some deep manure right here."

"Great ... I'll do just that. I can't wait to see what kind of manure we're getting into," I said, glancing in Kevin's direction.

"It's going to be okay, Connell, you have to trust me," Kevin whispered in my ear.

"Right, because that's worked out for me so far. Kevin, will you get a grip here, why do you all have weapons? We're in over our heads and need to get out of here. We still have a choice and we don't need to get wrapped up in their fantasy world," I pleaded with him.

"Connell, we've been friends for a long time, and all you ever talked about was fitting in. Well, I finally found a place where I fit in. Why can't you be happy for me?"

"Fitting in and breaking the law are two different things. What the heck do you think they're going to do with these weapons? Think, Kevin. Think!"

"I'm sorry, buddy, but I'm with them on this."

Kevin walked ahead of me and joined Lilly and Andie Rae in conversation, while I remained next to Bear. As Seventh Avenue filled up for the Friday night parties, we calmly walked through the crowd and turned left on Scott Street. Ahead on the right was an old abandoned warehouse with a sign hanging in the entrance way that said "Feast for the Forgotten." Heading towards this building were hundreds of what appeared to be poor or homeless people. It was clear to me that they were looking for a handout to help fill their bellies for the evening. I thought for sure this couldn't be our destination, but we walked right in with the rest of the crowd. Hayden positioned us at a table in the back corner of the building and told us to keep quiet. I glanced around, puzzled at the thought that they needed weapons to attend a charitable feast for the poor. There were rows of tables set with cauldrons full of soups and stews, and at the front was a stage. The most unusual thing about the place was that the roof was missing, but I couldn't see any type of threat.

With the sun now setting, people I took to be volunteers closed and latched the warehouse doors. To my surprise, Jack Alexander and his friends were the ones serving the food. All I could wonder was why they would give up their Friday night before football started for this. From the cheerleaders to the obnoxious bus driver, if they had anything to do with Jack and his friends at school, they were here. While Jack and his cronies continued to serve the people their food, a hooded figure came out of a back room, climbed up on stage and took a seat. The group of nut jobs I was with seemed very interested in this person and began to maneuver their weapons inside their coats. Hayden locked on him like a hound who just found a fox. He sneered at the hooded figure, apparently eager to attack. It looked like the only thing stopping him from leaping out of his seat was Andie Rae, who gently rubbed his hair and whispered something in his ear. It thought she was telling him to be patient, but I couldn't be sure.

With the sun now set, the hooded figure stood up, slowly walked up to the microphone on stage and began to speak to the crowd in a gravel-toned voice, one that I never heard the likes of before.

"Good evening and welcome to our feast. It's my hope that you now understand why I have asked all of you here tonight. As promised, our father, Kane, has provided another bountiful meal to help you make it through your next cycle," the hooded figure said in that deep, eerie voice.

"You do know what he's talking about, don't you?" Lilly asked me.

"Sure … the food," I replied.

Bear laughed and leaned in close. "I reckon you be right about one thing, he's chawing about the grub, but it ain't the grub on the table he talkin' about. It be us, he talkin' about."

I couldn't believe what I'd just heard. Their lunacy had reached a new level. This had gone far enough, and I decided to walk away from them. As I put my arms on the table and began to stand up, Bear grabbed me by my coat and, with little effort on his part, pulled me back down into my seat.

"Look, boy, it's fixin' to get muddy in here," he said, pointing at the white full moon overhead.

"Feast, my brothers and sisters, feast on what our father has delivered to us," the hooded figure said, laughing as he raised his head and hands towards the moon.

The people who had come to the warehouse to eat stood up and cheered their host. But something was happening around us. Jack and his crew screamed in anguish as they stared at the moon. Each one of their bodies convulsed as they mutated right before my eyes. They developed long snouts, sharp fangs, and hair growing all over their bodies. The crowd around me began to realize what was happening also, but it was too late; I couldn't believe my eyes—I was standing in a room filled with dozens of …

"Werewolves," Toby screamed while the entire team pulled out their weapons.

The crowd went into a panic as the beasts lunged in for the kill. Bear pushed me aside and pulled out his shotgun as he climbed on top of the table in front of us.

"*Yeee haww*! Come get some, boys," he shouted, discharging his weapon into the sea of monsters.

The rest of the group moved around the warehouse, shooting anything that moved on all fours. I gauged my surroundings: there was carnage everywhere. Man, woman or child, it made no difference; to these creatures all were merely a meal. Suddenly, I saw Hayden leap on the table in front of me and glare at the hooded figure.

"ENOCH!" he screamed, charging the hooded man.

Opening the back doors, allowing scores more werewolves into the warehouse, the hooded figure roared, "Hayden, how nice of you to join us."

The multitude of creatures pouring into the room didn't alter Hayden's course. He was picking up speed, clearly determined to get his hands on this person he called Enoch, and with every step, his appearance changed. His muscles tore at his clothes, his fingers were now massive claws, his body was covered in hair, and his mouth showed similar fangs to the other creatures in the room. However, there were differences between him and the werewolves. Hayden remained on two feet and he appeared to be fighting the creatures, not trying to devour the people. I immediately thought about the tale Andie Rae had told us back at Horror and Things and realized Hayden was the boy from the story.

Before he could get to Enoch, he was overwhelmed by beasts from every corner of the room. They lunged at him, clamping down on his flesh with their mighty jaws. Hayden let out a howl from time to time, and then pulled them off his body, leaving chunks of his flesh still in their mouths. It was apparent that they couldn't match his strength, but they made up for it with sheer numbers. Enoch disappeared through the rear doors as the werewolves continued their attack. Andie Rae, seeing Hayden in trouble, charged in with her weapon, spraying bullets across the room like a swarm of bees. Her aim was extremely accurate; she killed most of the vicious beasts without hitting Hayden at all.

With Hayden free, she retreated to her post, but I noticed her struggling with her gun. It appeared as if she was desperately trying to clear a jammed chamber. One of the remaining beasts was on top of her before she had time to react. Knocking her off her feet, the creature leaped on top of her. The only thing separating her flesh from its enormous fangs was her gun, which she was now using as a shield. Without thinking, I charged towards them. As I sprinted across the room, jumping over people lying in pools of their own blood, I felt my birthmark begin to burn. Glancing down, I noticed my arm glowing red through the sleeve of my trench coat. Based on tonight's events so far, it didn't surprise me that my birthmark would act up somehow, but I had to ignore it for now. Andie Rae was beginning to have trouble holding off the beast and, as its fangs got closer to her flesh, I could feel my legs moving quicker beneath me. As it lunged in for the kill, I flung my body forward, knocking it off of her before it had the chance to bite. It quickly got to its feet and stared at me with its yellow and black eyes. I had nowhere to go, and I had a feeling it knew it. If I'd only taken one of the weapons that had been offered to me earlier, but just like the rest of the day, I'd made a poor decision. The beast began to snarl and crouch down in preparation for its strike. I stared it down as I felt my heart begin to pound out of my chest. It opened its mighty jaw and leaped in for the kill. I screamed and closed my eyes—and heard gun shots ring out. I looked up to see Toby running towards me with one of the guns he'd offered me earlier, drawn and smoking. At my feet was the beast in a pool of its own blood.

"Thanks, Toby."

"Don't mention it, but next time, you may want to reconsider taking a gun."

With the lifeless wolf at my feet, I turned my attention to Andie Rae and quickly helped her over an enormous pile of dead bodies.

"Are you okay, Andie Rae?"

"Yeah … I'm fine. Thanks," she said awkwardly.

"Guys, I think it's time to leave," Doc pleaded, indicating another wave of creatures coming through the back door.

Andie Rae whistled, which told the rest of the team to begin heading towards the door.

"Bear, we need you. The latch on the door is too heavy," Doc yelled, while Toby and Kevin desperately tried to lift the large oak beam.

Rushing over to the door, Bear shoved all three of them out of his way. He dropped his shotgun, placed his shoulders under the oak beam and began to lift it from the latches on the door. With werewolves charging us, he hurled it their way, pinning many of them beneath its weight.

"Hayden, we fixin' to beat feet, come on you old dog, let's roll," Bear barked at Hayden, who in turn reluctantly retreated.

Kevin and Doc covered us as we exited the warehouse. One at a time we ran out of the door, Hayden changing back to his human form when he hit the street. Bear and Hayden began to push the doors closed before Doc and Kevin were in the clear.

"Come on guys, we're all out, move it," I shouted to get their attention.

They both rushed towards the door with the creatures snapping at their feet. The pair leaped out of the small opening, straightened up, and helped the rest of us try to secure the door. Kevin produced a metal rod he'd brought with him to latch the outside of the door. Just as he went to put it in place, the monsters attacked all at once, pushing the door open a crack, which exposed Kevin for a split second; a second was all it took. Before we could shove the doors closed, one of the things latched on to Kevin's foot, bringing him to the ground.

"Help me ... *help me!*" Kevin screamed as he was dragged back inside.

"*Kevin!*" I shouted, diving for his hand.

"Don't let me go, Connell ... please," he pleaded, panic in his eyes.

There were too many of them and they were too strong. I lost grip of my friend's hand, and he disappeared into the dark warehouse as the others slammed the door shut. Toby picked up the metal rod and jammed the doors with it. Lilly was beside herself, screaming for Kevin; Andie Rae pulled her away.

"We're leaving," Hayden commanded.

Everyone ran back towards Seventh Avenue. Everyone except for me. I didn't move; I couldn't move. I was in complete shock at what had just happened … my best friend since kindergarten was gone. Screaming at me to come on, Bear hurried over, grabbed me by the coat and flung me over his shoulder.

When we reached Centro Ybor City, he put me down, and we made our way back to Horror and Things. With all of us inside, Hayden slammed the door and locked it. Lilly fell into Andie Rae's arms, crying for my friend, who we could only think was dead. I collapsed into a chair by the window rubbing my birthmark, trying to come to terms with what I'd just experienced.

"Looks like all of those people weren't killed … look at the moon," Doc said, pointing out the red color that overpowered the once bright white sphere.

"Great, more of those things to kill in another month," Toby said, unloading his trench coat onto the bar.

"You still think we're all nuts, pansy?" Hayden asked me as he passed.

I didn't reply. I couldn't reply. Mentally exhausted, I stared at Andie Rae comforting her sister, as the others joined Toby at the bar and began to unload their weapons.

Chapter Four
Detention

The aroma of bacon was always enough to get me out of bed and ready to start the day. Even after experiencing the horrific terror in that warehouse, it was no different that morning. Rising out of the most uncomfortable chair I have ever slept on, I stretched and made my way towards the bar. Andie Rae was behind the counter, frying bacon. With no one else in sight, it would have been the perfect opportunity to make a dash away from this asylum, but I had to admit that after last night's events, I had become its newest inmate.

"Where is everyone?" I asked, taking a seat at the bar and rubbing my face.

"They're all in the back talking about our next move."

"How's Lilly?

"She's as well as can be expected. The bigger question is— how you are?"

The question hit me like a ton of bricks. I really hadn't taken time to absorb what had happened to Kevin. After almost fifteen years together, he was gone. I put my head down and placed my hands on my forehead as my stomach dropped to my feet.

"I don't know, to be honest. My world was turned upside down once again last night—I mean, I still can't believe Kevin is gone. It just seems like a really bad dream I can't wake up from. I don't know what to think or feel."

Andie Rae reached out to me and cradled my face with her soft hands. It was the touch of someone who seemed to know exactly how I was feeling, but I couldn't understand how. She raised my face so she could see my watering eyes and simply smiled at me.

"I'm so sorry about your friend. He was a really good guy. But right now, all you can do is take care of yourself and keep your head straight, and I think some food should help with that."

I nodded my head in agreement while wiping the tears from my eyes. She turned to the frying pan and removed the last few pieces of bacon. Then, she put the huge platter of perfectly fried pig on the counter next to the rest of the food she'd prepared.

"I'd get as much bacon as you want now, because when Bear gets in here, it will all be gone," she said, handing me a plate.

Selecting the crispest pieces of bacon, I said, "Can I ask you a question?"

"I guess you can."

"How did you ever get mixed up with this mess?"

There was a long silence as she started to put her plate together. I thought I may have just stumbled upon the reason moments earlier because she could relate to how I was feeling.

"I don't really like to talk about that."

"Come on, if anyone could understand, it's me. After all, you just saw what type of night I had. I promise I'll be on my best behavior," I said, crossing my heart with my fingers.

I could see the hesitation on her face. I wasn't sure if it was because she didn't trust me or if she still struggled with whatever she was holding inside. Looking at me, she eventually let out a deep sigh, put her plate down and took a seat at the bar.

"Fine … I'll tell you. But you promised your best behavior."

I raised my hand quickly and put it over my heart. "I promise."

"Okay. About five years ago my family and my boyfriend, Peter, were out celebrating my parents' anniversary. It was a wonderful evening, filled with laughter, love, and entertainment. Towards the end of the night, I felt sick and asked my family if we could head home before the end of the party. Of course they all agreed, so we began to walk towards our car, and I remember my mother pointing out how bright the full moon was that night. When we stopped to take a look, we heard their growls. My father and Peter thought they were stray dogs and stood in front of us, shouting at them to leave and throwing rocks at them. When the werewolves attacked, it took them mere seconds to kill both of them. I can remember my mother screaming as my father's blood splattered all over her. When the big one lunged for me and Lilly, Mom shoved us aside, and then, her screams just stopped. I covered Lilly with my body, trying to shield her from what was happening. I lay on top of her crying, praying that this was a bad dream, and I would wake up. I remember feeling the heat of their breath on the back of my neck as they stood over us. That was when my prayers were answered.

Hayden appeared and saved us from those monsters. I can still picture sitting up and watching him change back into his human form. I was cold, scared, and in shock. He wouldn't let me see my parents or Peter. Instead, he brought us here, and we've been with him ever since."

"I'm so sorry, I had no idea—"

"No idea that I caused the death of the people I loved," she said, cutting me off while wiping away her tears.

She stood up and walked over to the cooler and pulled out some orange juice. I didn't know what to say to her. The silence in the room was awkward, at best.

"Look, I'm sorry. Let's just drop it, okay," she said, returning to the bar with the juice. "By the way, thanks for saving me last night—that was pretty amazing what you did,' she said, pouring me a glass.

"Oh that, it was nothing … I mean … it was something, but—is it me or is it getting hot in here?" I asked, stumbling over my words.

Andie Rae simply smiled and turned to get more plates out, as the scent of the bacon triggered the rest of the gang to join us from the back room. They all piled around the bar and rushed to grab some bacon before Bear got there.

"There ain't nothing like eating some pig first thing to fix ya up right for the day," Bear said, seizing the rest of the bacon from the bar.

"So, pansy, what now? Are you going to run home and never look back?" Hayden asked, taking a seat at the end of the bar.

"Hayden, give the boy a break, he went through a lot last night," Doc interjected.

"Can't the pansy speak up for himself, Doc?" Hayden mocked.

Fed up with Hayden's crap, I threw my fork down and turned my stool towards him in disgust. "What's your problem with me? You've been on my case since I walked into this joint."

"My problem is that you've been lifted up on a pedestal by these guys, and you've done absolutely nothing to deserve it. Just because you have a mark that a book claims is the sign means nothing to me. I think you'll turn your back on us the first chance you get, just like you did last night."

I stood up and began to walk towards Hayden. "What are you trying to say?"

"I'm saying you're a coward. Why don't you tell us why you let go of your friend so easily," he countered, standing up.

"I lost grip of his hand. If I were you, I'd watch what you say next," I warned, pressing my head up against his.

"If I were you, I would back away from me, now."

"Or what, Hayden, are you going to lift your leg and take a piss on me, like the dog you are?"

That comment pushed Hayden over the edge, just like I thought it would. He growled and shoved me with all his might. The blow sent me soaring into a bookcase at the other end of the bar. As I lay below a pile of books and broken pieces of wood, dazed from the blow, I felt my birthmark begin to burn once again. It started to glow red, just like when I saved Andie Rae. As Hayden approached the pile of rubble I was under, I used the opportunity to surprise him. I leaped forward and tackled him to the ground and began to pummel his face with my fist. All the anger I had trapped inside from losing Kevin, my parents' deaths, and my grandmother's illness came pouring out. After a series of blows, I finally drew blood from his lip and could tell he was struggling to stop me. In pure desperation, he stretched out his arm and grabbed me by the throat. The power he had was indescribable. He dragged himself to his feet, blood dripping from his mouth, and heaved me up in the air by the throat, squeezing with all his might. While I gasped for air, I vaguely saw Andie Rae rush over to him and begin stroking his hair and whispering in his ear. He dropped me to the ground and returned to his seat at the end of the bar.

While I lay on the ground, struggling to catch my breath, Lilly and Doc rushed over to me.

"Are you okay?" Lilly asked.

"Let me take a look at you," said Doc.

"Guys, I'm fine, just give me a second," I pleaded, picking myself off the ground. I didn't want their help.

Everyone returned to their seats and continued to eat as if the altercation hadn't happened. Everyone except for Bear.

"Well, butter my butt and call me a biscuit. That boy just whupped your tail, Hayden."

"Shut up, Bear, he just caught me off guard," Hayden responded, wiping his mouth.

"If you asked me, I reckon he was having more fun with your face than a tornado in a trailer park," Bear countered.

This caused Toby and Doc to erupt in laughter.

Aggravated, Hayden threw his juice across the bar and stormed off to the back room. I was still rubbing my throat; Lilly handed me an ice pack for the bruises on my neck from Hayden's death grip.

"Shouldn't someone go talk to him?" I asked.

"No, he needs to blow off some steam. He'll be okay," Lilly said.

"I have never seen any one thing be able to match up to Hayden before. No man, no animal, and no werewolf. The more I learn about you, the more amazed I become," Toby said.

"Toby's right. I think that's what has Hayden up in arms. He doesn't know what to think of you, and he's having trouble coming to terms with the idea that you may be the one the Elders spoke of. For so long, it was all on his shoulders and now, to have the end in sight, well, it has to be quite perplexing," Doc added.

Frustrated, I dropped the ice bag on the bar and shook my head. "End in sight? Guys, he's right, I'm no savior, I have no idea what I'm doing, nor do I have any special powers."

"No special powers? You just took down a wolf man with little effort and drew blood. Nothing in existence besides another wolf man has the power to do that. You just haven't discovered how to use it yet," Lilly said.

"Then why have I never been able to tap into that power before last night?"

The room grew silent as each one of them pondered the question. It seemed like I just tossed a kink in their ideas of me being the savior. Then Doc spoke up.

"Maybe you needed to begin to believe in it first, and it took seeing the werewolves for you to begin that process. However, only Hayden would know for sure," he said.

"Great, so the only guy that can help me with this hates my guts."

"He doesn't hate you, Connell, he's envious of you," Andie Rae said.

I shook my head in disbelief again as I reapplied the ice pack to my throat. "Envious? He has a funny way of showing it if you ask me."

"Do you know how I got him to let you go? I reminded him of Kane, and that you were the one he needed to defeat him. He knows he doesn't have that power, but you do. Otherwise, you'd be dead right now, honey," she explained.

"Give him some time to take it in—he'll come around. After all, he's been waiting six thousand years for his revenge. Now that you're here, he knows the final showdown is looming, and he will not jeopardize that because of how he feels about you," Doc said.

The grandfather clock by the front door chimed; it was eight in the morning. The sound of the bell reminded me about the other asylum I was a member of and how I was supposed to be in detention in the next sixty minutes. Considering the circumstances surrounding the last twenty-four hours, I would've skipped out, but I knew Mr. Farley would have me suspended for sure. I couldn't allow that to happen, knowing Jack and his cronies were the key to figuring out our next move and finding out what happened to Kevin.

"Guys, I have to get going," I said, standing up.

"Where do you think you're going?" Toby asked.

"I have detention. I got to be at Chamberlain before nine."

"So let me get this straight. After last night, you're worried about school? Boy, you're nuttier than a porta potty at a peanut festival," Bear said.

"Guys, listen … last night, those people serving the food, a lot of them go to my school."

Everyone in the room stopped what they were doing and stared at me. I thought this would be common knowledge, since Lilly attended Chamberlain, but even she was taken off guard.

"Lilly, you should know that," I said.

"Connell, I don't go to Chamberlain. After Kevin told me about your birthmark, I really wanted to meet you. It was his idea for me to pretend to be a student and come to the school. He said it was

47

the easiest way to do it. I never stepped foot in that school before, and I was only there for lunch that day," she said.

"If they're werewolves, one of them must have spotted you last night before they transmuted. That means that you'll be in danger there," Doc said.

"It could give us the advantage we're looking for. I know Hayden has an informant, but watching these kids may provide us some additional information," Toby said.

"I agree, but he can't go by himself," Andie Rae said.

Everyone nodded in agreement, and I could tell they were all deep in thought. Andie Rae looked around the room at each one of her team and paused when she got to Bear. She smiled radiantly. "Bear, get dressed. Looks like you have detention."

Andie Rae gave me a change of clothes and a toothbrush so that I could freshen up before Bear and I took off for Chamberlain High. While I got ready, I could hear Bear ranting and raving about having to go and that he thought Toby should be the one stuck doing this. He carried on until I heard Hayden's voice, and all went silent. After a moment or two, there was a knock on the bathroom door.

"Hey, boy, I'll be outside waiting on ya," Bear shouted.

Whatever Hayden said to him worked because I didn't hear another peep out of him. I met Bear in front of Horror and Things and followed him over to his vehicle. It was massive, with wheels that would rival any monster truck I had ever seen. It was candy apple red, with lightning bolt decals down the side. The words "Bad

Moon Rising" were woven into the lightning. After climbing to the top of the truck and jumping in, I found the entire interior covered in fur. I rubbed it, trying to figure out what kind it was, as Bear started the engine.

"I skinned me one of them critters and used its hide to cover my buckets. You have to admit, boy, my truck is purtier than a mess of fried catfish," Bear declared while we roared down the street.

All I could do was laugh at him as he turned on "Let Your Love Flow" from the playlist on his phone. Bear had to be the most interesting person I had ever had the opportunity to meet, by far. He told me all about himself in the time it took us to get from Ybor City to Chamberlain High School. He never knew his father, and he lived with his mother in a trailer up in Land O'Lakes. His story was very similar to Andie Rae's. A werewolf murdered his mother in front of him as he unloaded his shotgun into it. At that time, he had no idea that he needed silver bullets to kill it, so his shells had no effect on the monster. He told me that when his ammo ran out he beat it in the head with his shotgun until it broke in two. Defenseless, the beast was able to trip him up and went in for the kill just as Hayden appeared.

"Ever since then, Hayden and I have been best buds. I like that old dog, he's a good guy. Heck, I can get where he's coming from. My momma was killed just like all his kin. I reckoned we could help each other out, and we've been together ever since," Bear concluded, pulling into the school parking lot.

I dismounted the massive truck and looked around. The mighty Chief with his unemotional expression was still on guard, protecting the sacred ground of his people, the social outcasts. Besides the few cars that were in the parking lot, the place looked deserted. Jack's mustang caught my eye immediately, and then it hit me. How would he react to me? How would I react to him? I could feel my heart pounding in my chest with every step I took. Beads of sweat began to form on my forehead as I pondered all of the different scenarios that could unfold in the next few minutes. The only thing that allowed me to continue towards the door was the fact that werewolves couldn't change without the full moon. I knew I had about a month before I would have to confront the furious beasts that took my best friend.

As we entered the main hall, I could see Mrs. Perry checking people in. While we stood in line, I wondered if any of them had seen me last night.

"Good morning, Connell," she said, checking my name off the list.

"Morning, Mrs. Perry."

"Are you okay?" she asked.

"Yeah, sure. Why do you ask?" I said; I felt suddenly nervous.

"You seem preoccupied. I wanted to make sure you weren't getting mixed up in something you should avoid," she said, scanning me up and down.

"Well, Jack and his crew are here and I'm not their favorite person."

"Why is that?" she asked.

"Let's just say I run my mouth too much," I said, smiling.

"Please go inside and take a seat. There must be no talking, so you should be able to stay out of trouble with them today. I'll give you further instructions once I finish checking everyone in," she added.

I made my way into the cafeteria while Bear tried to persuade Mrs. Perry that he was supposed to be there, regardless of what her list said. Jack and his associates were all huddled in the corner together. The moronic mob were chatting amongst themselves, Jack flirting with Tammy, the co-captain of the cheerleading squad. She was the most beautiful girl in school. She had blue eyes, long blonde hair, and long tan legs that never seemed to end. When I entered the torture chamber, they all went silent and looked up at me. Their stares felt like daggers, plunging deep into my soul. On the far side of the lunch room were my kind, the outcasts, but they continued to look down and doodle so that they wouldn't draw attention to themselves.

"Well, well, well … Connell Maxwell. I thought we were going to have to wait till Monday to catch up with you, but I guess luck was on our side," Jack said, and they all stood up. "Looks like you decided to get involved with something that wasn't any of your business, and now you'll have to pay for it."

"Jack, I know what you are … all of you. Don't—"

"Don't what, Connell? Are you going to tell on us? Who would believe a story like that? You listen to me, you little worm—you're going to pay for what you and your friends did last night. I'm just surprised you had the nerve to show up here all by yourself."

They circled me and moved in closer. Right now, I wished Mr. Farley did have this weekend instead of Mrs. Perry. While he was a total lurch, he wouldn't put up with this crap at all. As Jack reached for my shirt to deliver my second beating of the year, he paused as he heard a loud commotion coming from the hall.

"That's right honey, you go ahead and go check your computer for my name. I'll be in here waiting on ya with the rest of them folks," Bear said, entering the room and catching everyone's attention.

"Woo wee! It smells like wet dog in here," he joked, making his way towards me. "What's up, slick?" he asked Jack, getting between us.

"I don't know who the you are, but I'd watch your mouth if I were you," Jack said.

"Boy, you must be dumber than a barrel of spit and half as useful. Why you bowing up on me like a cat on Halloween? You don't know me from a hole in the ground. If ya don't back down, its fixin' to get ugly in here real quick," Bear said, spitting juice from his chaw onto Jack's shoes.

"What's going on in here?" Mrs. Perry demanded to know as she entered the room with a bunch of paperwork.

"Nothing, Mrs. Perry, just a big misunderstanding. Right, Jack?" I said.

"Right … just a big misunderstanding," Jack repeated as his mob returned to their seats.

"Mr. Maxwell. A word please?" she said.

I walked over to Mrs. Perry, and the sweet demeanor she was known for swiftly morphed into that of a witch.

"I asked you if you were getting involved with things you shouldn't, and it is clear you lied to me. I am very disappointed in you."

"It's really nothing, Mrs. Perry, I promise," I pleaded.

"Not another word and take a seat," she responded.

I plopped into my seat while Mrs. Perry passed out booklets for all of us to work on for the rest of the morning. The subject of our essay dealt with being a productive member of society and how this experience would help us improve our chances of succeeding in life. I couldn't help thinking that Mr. Farley had personally made this one up just for me. Bear continued to go over rosters with Mrs. Perry and assured her he was a new student. She allowed him to stay so he could get credit for attending and asked him to come find her next week to sort out his records.

The rest of the morning, as Bear would put it, moved as slow as turtles racing in molasses. Jack just drew pictures on the back of some type of flyer he had. They showed different scenes with my bowels spilled on the floor and my head missing. He would flash them my way every now and then to ensure I got the message. While his cronies laughed, I could see Tammy was getting annoyed at this childish behavior. Sometimes I thought she felt trapped by the classic high school expectation that the prettiest cheerleader had to date the quarterback. Another artificial rule that ticked me off and made me want to beat the heck out of its author. The clock slowly ticked away, and she was clearly bored out of her mind. Eventually she'd had enough and ripped the flyer away from Jack.

"Really, Jack, can you be any more immature," she groaned.

"What, are you some type of nerd lover now?" he responded.

Picking her stuff up along with the flyer, she snapped back, "Sometimes I really cannot stand you."

Tammy made her way over to a table by herself with the flyer folded between her books. She spent the rest of the morning quietly working on the assigned essay. Bear, on the other hand, was sound asleep, snoring and drooling on himself. I simply sat, feeling the stare of Jack's pride piercing through me. I kept my head down and worked on my essay only because I didn't want to end up back here next week for not doing it. I glanced over at Tammy from time to time to see what she was going to do with that flyer. I was sure it held a clue or something that could help out the gang back at the shop.

When midday was finally upon us, Jack and his crew were allowed to leave first. Mrs. Perry, while new to Chamberlain, was a very smart woman. She knew what they did to people like me, and, on most days, she was very protective of us. When they got up to leave, I locked in on Tammy, who crumpled up the flyer and threw it into the trash can on her way out. I could not believe my luck. When Mrs. Perry saw those idiots drive off from the windows, she excused the rest of us. I had to nudge Bear a few times; he was still out cold. As he rubbed his eyes and wiped his mouth, I hurried over to the trashcan.

"What do you have there, slick?" Bear asked, walking up to me.

While I was frantically uncrumpling the flyer, I whispered, "I think this is the clue we've been waiting on."

"How so?" Bear asked.

"While you were fast asleep, Jack had it and was drawing pictures on it. Tammy took it off him and threw it out," I said scanning the flyer. "Hot dang, here it is: Feasts with the Beasts."

"Dang, son, aren't you slicker than the grease of a b-b-cue biscuit." He chuckled.

"Thanks … I think?" I said.

"Come on, boy, let's get this back to Hayden and the gang," he said, pushing the doors to the cafeteria open.

We jumped back into his truck, turned on his tunes and howled as we tore out of the parking lot. While we made our way back to the shop to share the news, Bear was as lighthearted as always, singing his heart out to whatever was playing. Blowing his horn, we swerved around cars that were going too slow for him.

Chapter Five
Complications

The next twenty-eight days were absolutely miserable. All of the events from my first weekend with the gang caught up with me. I was full of every type of emotion that could be mustered. It felt like I was trapped in the grasp of a boa constrictor that was squeezing the life force from my body. The mayhem surrounding my life had me depressed and full of rage at the same time. There were no safe havens anymore; even the Chief's Head had become a center of interrogation by my fellow misfits on the whereabouts of Kevin. His loss was the toughest thing for me to absorb out of everything that had transpired. Seeing Mrs. McCool so distraught—and not telling her about that night—weighed heavily on my mind. She had faith that he would turn up just fine, and it was destroying me to know that he had been slaughtered because I couldn't hold on.

Jack and his mob didn't make it any easier. I knew they had the information I wanted about Kevin—what had happened to him and where his remains were located—but there was no way they would tell me. Even if they did, what good would it do? Besides, they were already keeping me busy by stepping up their attacks every chance they got. They were constantly reminding me that every day brought them closer to revenge. They promised me my death would be slow and painful, but they could have no idea that the process was well under way. If they were to kill me, it would save me from the anguish that surrounded me.

Mr. Farley was another source of discomfort for me. He never got over how I beat him that first day of school and had made me pay for it ever since. I had to admit that he was the least of my problems, but his gift of hurling insults was improving with each class period. In fact, he called me things I had to look up to fully grasp their meanings. Ignoring him had become my best course of action. While he screamed, turned red, and bulged his eyes at me, I just looked past him and tried to think about the only thing that had been a positive in my life lately: the guys at the shop.

The biggest shocker of them all was how crazy Mrs. Perry was acting after she accused me of lying to her. I constantly found her following me around school, pulling me aside to bombard me with questions about Bear, since he never showed up – where I knew him from and who else I was hanging around with. The more I played dumb, the more annoyed she got. It was so bad she actually called my grandmother, who had no idea what was going on at the school for much of the time. She was so sick. The stress was coming at me from all directions, and I felt like I was about to go insane.

When the bell rang to end the school day, my feet couldn't move fast enough. I just wanted to get away from it all. Jack and his abuse, Mr. Farley's insults, and the grilling's from the outcasts and Mrs. Perry had me at my breaking point. Bear and Lilly had met me out front every day since I returned to school for safety. They must have been able to tell that with each day that passed, I was becoming more miserable and annoyed at the entire situation. Today, I didn't say a word all the way to the shop, and, once we arrived, I just threw my books and took a seat in the corner chair. I didn't want to speak to anyone, and I didn't want to be bothered, either.

It was over an hour before anyone spoke to me. They were all in the back room talking about our next move, I was sure. I could hear Andie Rae arguing with Hayden about something, and, knowing what a lunatic he was, I knew it had to be an assignment she didn't think was a good idea. After a few rounds of going back and forth, they went silent. I could hear footsteps heading my way, so I now knew his plan included me.

"Hey pansy … get up," Hayden said.

I rolled my eyes. "What do you want, Hayden?"

"Looks like you have a lot on your mind. I'm sending you to Bear's place up in Land O'Lakes for some rest and relaxation with Andie Rae. You need to spend tomorrow getting your head back in the game."

"Why do you care where my head is?"

Hayden rubbed his head in frustration and let out a big sigh. "The only thing I care about is the full moon, and we have one coming in two days. If you can't get your act together, you'll be no use to us."

I looked out the window and tried to ignore him altogether. I didn't really care what he was saying—I was still feeling sorry for myself. Shaking my head, I turned back towards him.

"What if I don't want to go?"

"I'll make you go," Hayden replied with a growl.

Looking past Hayden, I saw Andie Rae appear with two duffle bags. It then sunk in that I was going to get to spend this time with her all by myself. That idea perked me up, even though I knew that was what they'd been arguing about. I was sure she didn't want to go; however, I wasn't going to let this opportunity slip past me.

"Okay, Hayden, I'll go ... when do we leave?" I asked, trying to hide my new-found excitement.

"Right now. Remember, don't stop for any reason. Bear's place already has everything you need. Stay put and get your head back in the game. Otherwise, come the full moon, you may lose it," he said, walking away.

"What's with the grin?" Andie Rae asked.

"Nothing ..." I responded, trying to get myself under control.

"Nothing? Right. Don't you be getting any ideas. I'm only doing this so you don't get yourself or one of us killed," she said, tossing me my bag as we headed towards the door.

I followed her out of the shop feeling much better than I did when I arrived. After loading our bags in the trunk, I jumped into the passenger seat and rubbed my hands together in anticipation of spending some one-on-one time with her. For the first time in weeks,

I stopped thinking of all my problems and was excited for the here and now. It seemed that she read my thoughts, though, and was already reinforcing the mental wall she'd built around herself since her journey with Hayden's team began.

The drive to Bear's place took longer than I hoped, and there wasn't much conversation between us. She made it abundantly clear that she was upset about being there, and I had to figure out a way to get her to lower her guard and let me in. I decided the best course of action was just to go and have fun, set no expectations, and avoid asking too many questions. I figured if I showed her a good time, her barriers would come down by themselves, and I could try when the opportunity presented itself.

Pulling off the interstate, we turned left down the main highway for about a mile. We took another left on a dirt road and headed deep into the tree line. The road twisted and turned every few minutes, driving us deeper into the woods and further away from society. I was starting to wonder where in the world we were heading when we cleared the tree line on the other side. We pulled up to a gate overlooking an enormous meadow with a white picket fence surrounding a large red barn. There must have been dozens of horses in the pastures, prancing around showing off their speed and agility. Andie Rae punched in the code to open the gate and continued up the driveway and around the barn. On the far side was a triple wide trailer in perfect condition. To be honest, this far exceeded my expectations when I considered how Bear carried himself.

"Well, we're here," she said, putting the car in park.

Sensing how uncomfortable she was, I turned in my seat to face her and put my hand on her shoulder.

"Andie Rae ... listen. I know you don't want to be here, but can we at least try to have a good time? I promise, no funny business, just fun ... what do you say?"

She looked out the window towards the horses for a few minutes before answering me.

"No funny business, right?"

"Scout's honor," I said, holding up three fingers.

"Okay, I can do that," she said. She opened the door and stepped out of the car.

I jumped out, grabbed my bag from the trunk and walked towards the trailer. Inside, it had the feel of a cozy and inviting old country cottage. As I walked through the living room, there were pictures all over of a woman with a much younger Bear. I assumed it was his mother whom he lost to one of the monsters so many years ago. She was so beautiful, full of life and happy. I couldn't help but think how much her loss must have affected Bear and that this place was his only connection to her.

"Hey, I'm going to take the bedroom down on the left. You can have Bear's room," Andie Rae said as she headed towards the kitchen.

When I opened the door to Bear's room, it was much more like him. The place was full of weapons, clothes were thrown all over, and his bed was outfitted in camouflage. I threw my bag on the bed, grabbed the broom in the corner, and swept the clothes on the floor into a pile in the closet.

"Do you want to help me make dinner?" Andie Rae shouted.

"Yeah, sure … I'll be right there."

I quickly looked myself over in the mirror to make sure my appearance was acceptable and did a quick breath check. Since everything seemed okay, I made my way towards the kitchen, reminding myself to stay in the safe zone and allow Andie Rae to open up on her own. After all, I had time, so there really was no need to push my luck the first night.

"Grilled cheese and soup okay with you?" she asked, spreading butter on the bread.

"Sure, it sounds great, but what can I do to help?"

"How about working on those cans of soup?"

I moved over to the counter, grabbed a couple of cans of soup, and opened them. Pouring them into the pot on the stove, my mind was racing, trying to think of something to say without making myself look like an idiot. I was drawing a complete blank, I could feel beads of sweat starting to form on my forehead, and I was quickly heading into a panic. I have no idea why, but I started to sing along to "Sweet Home Alabama" as it played on the radio. Andie

Rae chuckled at me while placing the cheese sandwiches in the frying pan.

"What do you know about Alabama?" she asked.

Stirring the soup, with no idea about anything to do with Alabama, I figured I would turn the tables. "What do *I* know about Alabama? What about you? While you look the part, what would make me believe it's for real?"

"Really, you just went there? Well, honey, I'm going to show you what Alabama is all about."

She turned up the radio as loud as it could go and started singing and dancing where she stood. For the first time since I'd known her, she seemed happy. We laughed and joked around with each other for the next hour or two, and enjoyed our dinner together. There was no stress for either one of us, just relaxation and fun. Part of me couldn't help but think that Hayden had sent her up here for herself and not to help me. Perhaps he had a soft side after all.

After dinner, we took our sweet tea and went outside to sit on the porch. I couldn't believe how beautiful it was. The sky was lit up by bright stars that seemed more prominent away from the city lights. At last, after they'd built up over the last month, I could feel my stress levels declining. The relief was overwhelming, and I couldn't help but think part of it was because of who I was with.

"Hey, thank you so much for coming up here with me. I really needed this."

She smiled, picked up her glass, and took a sip of her sweet tea. "To tell you the truth, I think I needed this as much as you did."

It seemed that she wanted to say more, but she stopped herself. I wasn't going to push her to find out what was on her mind. Instead, I thought it would be best just to keep the conversation simple.

"So what do you want to do tomorrow?" I asked.

She shrugged her shoulders and turned her attention towards the horses prancing in the moonlight. The smile returned to her face as she looked very excited. She turned back towards me and put her tea on the table between us.

"Let's go," she said, grabbing my hand and pulling me off the porch.

"Where are we going?"

"Come on, city boy. It'll be okay, I promise."

She picked up her pace and we jogged towards the barn next to the horses. I started to get an unsettled feeling in my stomach as I thought I knew what she had in mind. She opened the barn doors to reveal a ton of boots, saddles, blankets, reins, and bits. She let go of my hand and moved towards the saddles hanging on their stands. She brushed her hand gently across the smooth leather as she made her way around them. Facing me now with that same playful smile she gave me a quick wink.

"This is what we're going to do tomorrow if you're up for it?"

I was silent for a few seconds. I knew as much about riding horses as I did about building a space rocket, but there was no way I was going to let her down after this major breakthrough. How bad could it be—you get on one, kick it one or two times, and it goes forward.

I walked up to the saddle where she was standing, leaned over, and put my face close to hers. I whispered softly, "You're on."

She laughed at me and pushed me back by the chest. "Sounds like a date. Meet me back here at eight in the morning, and we'll see what you got," she said, dancing around the saddle and heading towards the barn doors.

I followed her with my eyes, and she stared right back at me. When she reached the barn doors, she stopped and leaned on one, looking at me. "Thank you for a wonderful night, Connell. I haven't had this much fun in a long time. Good night."

"Good night, Andie Rae," I shouted as she turned the corner and walked out of sight.

"A date," I whispered to myself. I turned back towards the saddle and leaned on it in disbelief. "Now all I have to do is not make a fool out of myself tomorrow," I concluded, running my hands through my hair.

I closed the barn doors and made my way back to the house. When I got inside, I latched the bolts and headed to Bear's room. After a quick shower, I jumped into bed and did my best to try and fall asleep after an amazing evening.

The next morning came quickly, and I was exhausted from lack of sleep. I was convinced the grumbling in my stomach was a combination of hunger and nervousness. I pulled myself out of bed and stumbled towards the bathroom to freshen up. While I brushed my teeth, I was going through my potential next steps in my mind. Did I ask her out on an official date if the day went well, or did I take what she gave me and call it a victory? My frustration was at an all-time high; I'd never had this type of problem before, and I only wished I had someone to talk my options over with. I wiped my mouth and chuckled at that thought. The only one I would've possibly shared this with was Kevin, and I could only imagine the bad advice he would have given me. Looking down at my birthmark, it finally hit me how much I missed my awkward, comical, and loyal best friend. My eyes began to water, and I knew I had to get a grip of myself. I switched my thoughts to something I really enjoyed: picking out my outfit. Since this had been declared a date, I had to look the part, but what I wore also had to fit in with with horseback riding. After looking through the bag she'd given me, it became clear that my choices were very limited. Blue jeans and any color tee shirt I wanted was all I had to work with. I decided to let fate decide and just reached in with my eyes closed, and I pulled out a royal blue tee.

After getting dressed, fixing my hair, and scanning over to make sure I looked good, I headed towards the kitchen to grab some breakfast. When I entered the room, there was a pair of black boots sitting on the counter next to a plate of eggs and bacon with a sealed envelope. I took my shoes off and slid the boots on. They felt awkward at first, but after a few moments of walking in them, I found them to be surprisingly comfortable. I took a seat at the bar and picked up the white envelope. On the back of it was an imprint of Andie Rae's lipstick and the words "Sealed with a lick because a kiss just won't stick." I snickered and tore it open. I pulled out the letter. It simply said "Thank you for a wonderful night! Now hurry up and eat so we can get to riding!"

I choked down my food as quickly as I physically could so that I wouldn't disappoint her. Breakfast was gone in five seconds, and it felt like I cleaned up in five more. I hurried out the door, and I could see her saddling up the second horse. As I made my way across the field, I could feel my stomach in my throat; the idea of riding these animals was now a reality.

After kneeing the horse in the gut while she tightened the saddle, Andie Rae turned to see me slowly approaching. "Good morning—I was beginning to think you ran away on me or something,"

I approached the white stallion and started to pet his snout. "I will admit that I'm nervous, but there's no way I'd pass this up."

Bending over a bucket of brushes, she paused, cocked her head, and looked at me. "Really, why is that?"

"Because this is what you wanted to do and that matters to me. Besides, when else is a guy like me going to get to spend an entire day with someone as beautiful as you?"

There was an awkward silence for a minute. I could not believe what I'd just said; I was afraid to look at her—I thought I was going to vomit my breakfast right there on the spot.

She laughed as she picked up a brush and turned back towards the black stallion. "You know, sometimes you're just too much, but I think it's really sweet."

I let out a sigh of relief at her response.

I walked over and patted the horse on the neck. "Who takes care of the horses for Bear?"

"He has a friend who takes care of them when he's away from the place," she answered.

"Are you ready to go?" I asked.

"Just about." She threw the brush back into the bin next to her.

She turned her back to me once again and I could tell she was pretending to buckle some bags on the saddle. "I packed us some lunch and drinks in our saddlebags. I was thinking we could have a picnic once we get over to the lake if that's okay with you?"

I jumped up and raised my fist in the air. She was worried that I wouldn't want to. That was the most welcome news I could have received. This trip was totally beating my expectations. I got control of myself as she turned around to face me. I realized I forgot to answer her: what a dummy.

"We don't have to," she said, sounding disappointed.

"No, that would be amazing," I replied hysterically.

She tilted her head to the side and asked, "Are you sure?"

I hurried over to her and put my hands on her shoulders. "There's nothing I'm more positive about right now in the entire world. It's going to be an incredible day."

She shot her famous smile at me one more time and answered, "Well, what are we waiting for?"

"Let's get going." I turned back towards the white stallion.

Andie Rae jumped up into the saddle with no problem whatsoever. She had her horse away from the fence, walking in circles while waiting on me to join her. After loosening the reins from the post, I made my way to the left side of the horse. I could feel Andie Rae staring at me to see how well I could handle myself. I jumped up in one quick and smooth motion and the horse began to move towards the trailhead.

"Whoa, big fella," I commanded, pulling back on the reins.

The horse started to spin in circles and pull its head down towards its chest. I tried my best to keep control of it, but it was like the horse could feel my lack of confidence and was competing with me to see who would be in charge. After a few kicks and jumps, we both found out who the winner of round one was: him.

Andie Rae trotted up to check on me. "Are you okay?"

Standing up and wiping the dirt off of me, I looked up at her with a smirk. "My ego hurts more than my butt does right now, but thanks for asking."

She laughed and spun her horse around to grab the reins of the white stallion. Bringing my opponent back over to me, she handed me the reins. "Come on, big boy, you can do it."

Embarrassed, I took a deep breath and jumped back on top of the horse. I could feel it wanted to go for round two, but Andie Rae, who was still beside me, showed me how to hold the reins and position my body. The horse calmed down, and I was able to finally control it with basic commands.

Breaking into a slow trot, I looked back at her and shouted, "Come on, we're wasting sunlight."

"You didn't just go there," she responded, breaking into a gallop to catch up with me.

The next few hours flew by as we rode deep into the woods. She taught me a lot about horseback riding and lured me into a few short races every now and then. For the first time in my life, I wasn't worried about what others thought of me, how I looked, or even if my birthmark was showing. It felt like the huge anvil that always weighed me down was lifted off my chest. I could feel what it meant to be free from all of a teenager's worries, and I loved every minute of it. There was no pecking order, no popularity contest, and certainly no bullies ready to beat on you because you happen to run with a certain crowd. It was just me and this beautiful girl galloping down a trail and enjoying each other's company.

As we cleared the tree line, we found ourselves in a large field with a big lake at the edge of it. We walked our horses down towards the shoreline and dismounted about thirty feet from the water. I have to admit that, while I never had a better morning, my butt was extremely happy to be out of that saddle.

This place was beautiful. The sun was shining, the sky was clear, and the water was crystal blue and inviting. Andie Rae took the horses and put them in a small corral that seemed to be built just for this purpose. While she got our lunch out of the saddlebags, I was hypnotized by her beauty. I wanted to tell her exactly what I was thinking, but I was too afraid the feeling was not mutual. Besides, I'd promised myself not to move on this too quickly. She came out of the corral and tossed me a blanket to spread out on the ground. We both sat on the blanket, and she started to sort out the food and drinks. The silence was awkward at best, but I took it as a sign that she was struggling to find what to say. Perhaps she was having the same thoughts I was.

I lay back on the blanket with my hands under my head and looked out to the horizon. "Beautiful," I said.

She turned her head quickly towards me as if she was in shock. "What did you say?"

"The view, it's just beautiful."

She put her head down and returned to sorting lunch. "I don't have much use for looking up at things in the sky when people mention them anymore."

Remembering what she told me about the night her family was killed, I realized what I'd done. "Hey, I'm sorry, I didn't think—"

She cut me off as she wiped a tear away from her face. "Forget it, okay? Let's just eat."

I turned on my side to face her, and she continued to sit Indian style. As she passed me my portion of lunch, I mentally ran through what I could do to get beyond the damage I'd just created. I looked around and decided I didn't want to bring any more attention to anything that had to do with scenery, so I did the only logical thing I could think of.

"Hey, can I get some ice in a bag for my butt?"

She stopped mid-chew and just stared at me. "What do you want?"

I had no choice at this point. I committed to the leap and I was all in. "You know, ice for my butt. It's really stinging from that saddle."

She covered her mouth so she wouldn't spit her food out as she laughed. Putting her sandwich down, she turned towards the small cooler bag that held our drinks, grabbed a handful of ice, and wrapped it in a towel.

"Here you go, champ—I forgot it's your first time."

I applied the bag of ice to my backside and held it there. "It's like that horse knew where every rock, bump, and hole was in the trail, and he was determined to make my life miserable."

"I'm just shocked it hurts that much. You seemed to be doing so well. I thought you were a natural."

"Well, I'm a quick learner when it comes to most things, but galloping for four plus hours was a little more than my backside could bear."

She shook her head and went back to eating. I knew I'd taken a big chance by talking about such a stupid topic, but it seemed to work. She let the whole horizon thing go. I learned a valuable lesson about her, and all the fun we had was not lost.

When we finished up lunch, she lay on her side and faced me. "I'm sorry about snapping back there. I guess I'm so used to being strong and numb that all the fun I had today caught me off guard."

I reached out to touch her hand, but she pulled it away from me. "Please, just let me finish."

"Okay, I'm sorry."

"Connell, you have really surprised me so far. When I first met you, I thought you were a jerk, but I can see you're so much more. But the last time I let people in and became close to them, bad things happened. The thought of that happening again really scares me."

I rolled onto my back and put my hands under my head. I had a few possibilities at this point—fight for what I wanted and risk losing everything or give her more time, which was the last thing I wanted to do. I really had few options and chose the safe and respectful route.

"Andie Rae, I'm not trying to push you into anything. I just want to hang out, enjoy your company, and unwind from all the craziness in our life. Like I said, my best behavior, nothing more and nothing less."

She turned to lay on her back and put her hands on her stomach. "Thank you so much for understanding, Connell. It really means a lot to me."

I had to admit that I'd made a lot of progress with her, just not as much as I hoped for.

After tidying up, we got the horses out of the corral and headed back to the barn. The ride home was okay, but for me, it seemed to have lost some of its luster. For the next four hours, we talked about this and that, nothing really of importance, and I just tried to keep a smile on my face. My mind was racing because I knew I was running out of time, and there was so much more work to do.

We got back to the barn, cleaned up the horses, fed them, and locked the barn up. My body was worn out from all the riding. Andie Rae took off her hat and rubbed her face with her arm. "Boy, I need a long, hot shower. Do you mind if we don't cook anything for dinner tonight? I think I'm just going to turn in early, if that's okay with you?"

I stopped on the porch, leaned against the handrail, and sighed. My time had just run out on me. "No, I'm good with that. It has been a long day. To be honest, I'm beat, and turning in early sounds like an excellent idea."

She turned and headed towards the door without saying a word. I didn't know what to think. The entire situation hadn't gone as I planned. I still wanted to tell her how I was really feeling, but after the lake, I knew that wouldn't be welcomed.

She stopped at the door, opened it, and turned to me. "Connell, I'm sorry I'm all messed up inside. I really did enjoy today, I'm just not ready to let anyone in. I have enough to worry about with Lilly—I can't handle losing anyone else I care about."

I jumped up on the banister and sat on it. I knew my frustration was showing on my face, but I had to put her needs in front of my wants. I said, "I totally understand. Don't worry about it. This was about having a good time, nothing more, nothing less, right?"

She smiled as she looked down and turned towards the doorway. "Right. Good night, Connell."

"Good night, Andie Rae."

After she was out of sight, I slammed my fist against the wood handrail in anger. I got up and entered the house. I locked the door and headed straight towards Bear's room. Too sick to eat, I decided to get a quick shower and call it a night. While I soaked under the hot, refreshing water, I couldn't believe I'd chickened out. It was right there for me to say, she gave me the opening and I blew it. Toweling off and throwing on some undergarments, I had to accept that it was over as we were heading back to the shop in the morning. I turned the light out, rolled over in bed, and faced the large window; I stared at the moon. It was bright and large. There was only a small sliver of it missing, one that would be there this time tomorrow night, along with whatever plan Hayden had cooking.

Chapter Six
Over the Edge

With the sun peaking over the horizon, I realized it was time to head back to reality, head back to face my enemies, head back—knowing I may never see another sunrise. Those thoughts overtook any worries I had about last night as I rolled out of bed and made my way towards the bathroom. I already knew what the guys were doing back at the shop: cleaning their weapons and getting ready to battle for their lives one more time. I didn't know how they did it month after month; perhaps they got numb to the idea that they were walking into death's door for a fight. Maybe the holes torn into their hearts from losing loved ones to those creatures removed their ability to think straight. I'd lost Kevin, and I'd come to accept that. But the fear was too new, the foe too massive to imagine getting to that point. Maybe Andie Rae was right—there was no time to care. It would only cloud your mind to the most important thing: self-survival. With these thoughts racing through my head, I felt sick to my stomach and was forced into submission to the porcelain bowl.

After washing up from my unpleasant episode, I took a quick shower, brushed my teeth, and got dressed. I grabbed my bag and headed to the main room to see if Andie Rae was ready to go. I saw her bag by the front door, so I dropped mine beside it and continued to the kitchen. She was sitting on a stool by the counter eating what appeared to be biscuits and gravy.

I plopped down next to her, grabbed a glass, and filled it with some orange juice. "Hey, good morning."

"Good morning. I made you some breakfast."

"No thanks, I'm not hungry," I said rudely.

She dropped her fork on her plate and swung around towards me. "Okay, I knew this was a bad idea. Connell, I thought we had an understanding—"

"This is not about you," I snapped back, cutting her off.

"Okay, big boy, what is it about then?"

I rubbed my face with my hands and let out the most sarcastic laugh I would muster. "Are you that unemotional? Do you not realize what we'll be doing in another eight hours or so? Your life, your sister's life, my life, all on the line. Is this just another day to you now?"

She got up and took her plate to the sink and began washing it. The silence puzzled me. After finishing the dishes, she shut off the water and dried her hands with a towel. Turning towards me, she ran her left hand through her blonde hair and she gave me the answer I expected.

"I guess the answer would be yes. It's what we do, it's who we are, and it's what you're becoming."

I slammed my glass on the counter and stormed out of the kitchen. "Great, I can't wait. I'll meet you in the car."

As I grabbed my duffle bag, I felt the hate for my birthmark boil within me. I never asked for this destiny, and I wasn't ready to lose my life over it. When I got to the car, I dropped my bag on the ground. The pent-up anger began to seep out of me and I lost control. I kicked my bag across the driveway and punched the car over and over. I turned and saw Andie Rae come out of the house and sprint towards me. My knuckles were bruised and bleeding from pounding the hard metal. Tears were streaming down my face and I yelled as loud as I could. She flung her arms around me and held me tight. I brought my bloody hands to my face and sobbed uncontrollably. She never said a word and neither did I. It seemed like I'd finally achieved what Hayden sent me up here to do: I dealt with my emotions and put them in check. I had no doubt in my mind—I just took another step closer to sealing my fate as one of them. When I calmed down, she let me go. I went over to my bag and retrieved a shirt out of it. I used it to wipe my face and hands. I picked my bag up, threw it in the back of the car and collapsed into the passenger seat. After a few minutes, Andie Rae tossed her bag into the back seat and got into the car. We didn't talk or even look at each other during the drive home. I shut my eyes and hoped, when I opened them again, I would wake up and return to my simple life of eating brown sack lunches under the Chief's Head.

We drove for well over an hour before she pulled the car over and turned off the engine. We were back at the shop, and it was time to prepare for tonight's events. Who knew what lunacy Hayden had waiting for us, but I needed to make things right with Andie Rae first. When she turned to reach into the back seat to grab her bag, I took a deep breath. I turned towards her, reached for her hand, and turned her gently to face me. The expression on her face shocked me. I'd thought she was upset with me about the entire situation, but she was smiling.

"I don't understand—I thought you would be upset with me?"

"Connell, why would I be mad at you? All you were doing was finally dealing with everything that's happen to you over the last few weeks." She turned my hands over and stroked my bruised knuckles. "I just envisioned it being expressed another way, that's all. You're a lot like Hayden, and in time, you will learn to do things … things I couldn't even begin to attempt. The world is depending on you—Hayden is depending on you."

"What about you? Are you depending on me?"

She pulled her hands away from me and I knew she could tell my question went much deeper than it appeared on the surface.

"Connell, life is too complicated, I'm too complicated. So much has already happened, and I can't be hurt again. Not like that."

I knew she was referring to our conversation last night about not seeing someone else she cared for get hurt. If I was going to get closer to her, I knew I had to respect that boundary.

"Hey, let's not worry about that right now. How about we both just try to survive whatever Hayden has cooking in his head for tonight? If we make it through that, we'll worry about tomorrow when the sun rises, okay?"

She smirked and nodded her head in agreement. "Thank you for understanding."

"No, thank you for getting me to this point. Now, how about we go inside and see what the guys are up too?"

She turned, grabbed my bag and handed it to me. After picking up her own bag, we left the car and headed towards the front door. When we entered the shop, Bear and Toby were behind the bar prepping their weapons. Andie Rae went straight towards the back room, and I wandered over to see what was going on.

"What's up, guys?" I asked, taking a seat at the bar.

Toby took off his glasses and rubbed the thick lenses against a handkerchief. Squinting, he held them above his head to make sure he'd got the smudge before returning them to his face.

"It's about time you got here. We're way behind schedule and could use some help."

I'd never seen Toby so vocal and annoyed. He turned his attention to the silver orbs in the crate next to him. He carefully started to hook them onto his vest, one at a time, shining them as he did so. I picked up a clip off of the bar and began to fill it with silver bullets. Bear, to the left of me, was also hard at work filling up as many clips as he could.

I leaned over towards him so Toby wouldn't hear us. "Bear, what's up with Toby and those silver orbs?"

Bear picked another clip, started loading it, and spat some of his chewing tobacco into the jug on the floor.

"I reckon he just wants to go out his own way, I suppose."

Bear always had his own way of explaining things, and today was no different. It was like he had his own language of sorts.

"Bear, how about in English this time so I can understand?"

"You know, boy, sometimes I think you be as sharp as a cue ball. The boy carries them orbs just in case one of them things gets a hold of him. You see, the orbs are his creation, grenade-type explosives. He figures if he gets overrun and has to check out of this fine place, he'll just pull the pin and see what happens next. Would make anything near him hotter than two hamsters farting in a wool sock."

I shook my head and chuckled. "Bear, thanks for that perfect picture. I don't think I'll ever get it out of my head."

He took a swig of his soda and spat out his juice one more time. "So, what did you think of my homestead. Purty, isn't it?"

"Yeah, it was awesome, and I loved all the pictures of you and your mom."

He continued to load clips and didn't acknowledge my comment. "Andie Rae, honey, how about fixin' us some grub for lunch. Lilly is okay, but she ain't no Betty Crocker."

It became clear to me that while it was okay for him to bring up the subject of his mom, he didn't appreciate it when others did. Everyone seemed to deal with this mess so differently, and being the new guy, I needed to learn to keep away from people's sensitive spots. Andie Rae came out from the back and started to make lunch for everyone.

"Bear, I appreciate that you love my cooking so much, but is there something wrong with your hands that you can't make it yourself?"

He erupted in laughter so hard he began to choke on his chaw. "Honey, that is the funniest thing I've heard in a while. Me cooking would go over like a pregnant pole vaulter—ain't gonna happen."

I just shook my head and continued my task. Andie Rae didn't find his remarks humorous at all. She rolled her eyes and continued to prepare lunch. Shortly after, Lilly, Doc, and Hayden came out from the back room. Hayden took his normal spot at the end of the bar, while Lilly and Doc joined the main group. With lunch now served, we all ate quickly and joked around with each other, trying to ignore what was coming up. Hayden never seemed to let his guard down. While we were all enjoying the time we had together, he kept to himself and picked at his food.

"Hey, Lilly, why does Hayden always stay to himself?" I asked quietly.

Lilly glanced over at him to make sure he was not paying attention to us, and then leaned towards me and whispered her answer.

"He knows people are going to die tonight. It weighs heavy on his mind, but he refuses to acknowledge it to the group."

"Why are you whispering?"

"Because if he knew we were talking about him, he would be really upset."

I leaned back in my chair and stared at him. Many thoughts went through my mind, and I figured since we never really got along anyway, I didn't have anything I to lose by breaking this rule.

"Hayden, what's your problem, man? Come on over and sit with us."

The room went silent, and all eyes shifted to Hayden for a response. He dropped his sandwich on his plate and gave me a blank stare.

"What's wrong with you? I thought we were a team. Why are you always moping around and putting on this stone-cold show? Get over yourself and get over here."

Hayden looked down at his plate and started to laugh. He stood up and began to make his way towards the table. It was clear he wasn't happy with me.

"Pansy, what makes you think you are part of this team? In fact, what makes you believe you can talk to me like I'm your buddy? When did this disconnect come into play?"

He stood over me while the team sat around us. I figured, what was one more fight before he told us his plan?

"Hayden, I don't have the energy or time to deal with your crap. If you want to go toe to toe, let's do it. Otherwise, shut up, sit down, and let's discuss our next move."

Immediately, everyone except Bear moved away from the bar. The room was silent. Hayden seemed to be deciding what his next move was going to be. He grabbed me by the shirt and pulled me up from my chair so quickly that I didn't have time to react. Bear jumped up as well and put his arms between us.

"Dang it, you two are acting madder than a pack of wild dogs on a three-legged cat. This fightin' is as worthless as chicken crap on a pump handle. We fixin' to be in a world of hurt, and the best thing y'all can do is tinker with each other. Get over it and let's get down to business, boys."

Hayden let go of me and nodded at Bear. I fixed my shirt and shut my mouth. The other team members gathered back by the bar and took their seats. Hayden went around the other side of the bar so that he was standing in front of us. He pulled out some notes from his pockets and placed them on the bar in front of him, including the flyer that Bear and I took from the trashcan at Chamberlain.

"Okay, I was able to confirm what the pansy thought. Tonight, the zoo over by Lowry Park in Tampa is having a huge fundraiser. There are going to be all kinds of people there. Perfect feeding opportunity and cover story. Some animals get loose in the zoo, eat a few people, and no one will suspect anything."

He picked up a map of the area and pinned it to the board behind him. We were split up into teams and assigned stations outside the zoo. He gave us strict orders not to engage until one of them struck first. The smell of blood would set off a frenzy that would blind their ability to run off when we started to fire our weapons at them.

I shook my head and waved my hands in disbelief. "Wait a minute, are you telling me that we are to let someone die? Just sit there and watch it happen?"

Doc leaned in towards me and tried to reason with me. "Connell, it's just like any other war—there will always be collateral damage. It's for the good of the cause. We'll be able to kill more of them by sacrificing the one."

I cocked my head sideways and looked at him. "So, Doc, you would still feel the same way if it was your family, friend, or girlfriend? I find that hard to believe … right, guys? You're with me, aren't you?"

The room was silent, and no one said a word to back me up. It was clear that this, too, was part of the indoctrination process of being one of Hayden's merry men.

"Okay, I get it, no problem. I'll just sit back and follow your lead."

"Good. That is all you need to do, and we will save a lot of lives tonight," Hayden responded.

I smirked and dropped my head in disbelief. This just didn't seem right, but it was clear I was in the minority on this one.

"Okay, everyone, finish loading up. We'll be moving out in a few hours," said Hayden.

We broke up and went back to our tasks, finishing the last of the details before we packed our gear into the cars. Toby came over to me and handed me a long, black trench coat, a silver combat knife and a Glock with multiple clips.

"I'm assuming you will take weapons this time," he said, smiling at me.

I didn't hesitate. If it weren't for Toby, I wouldn't be here at all.

"Yeah, I think I will this time around."

It was about one o'clock, ninety minutes before the full moon would be gleaming in the skyline. We divided up into the cars and headed towards Tampa. It was a quick thirty-minute ride over to the zoo. We took the interstate and got off at the Sligh Avenue exit, taking it all the way to North Boulevard where the zoo was located. We pulled into the parking lot, positioned ourselves outside the cars, and waited. The parking lot was filling up, and people were piling into the zoo. From old couples to young children, every age group was represented. Looking at all of those happy people, I wondered which would be the one sacrificed so willingly by the group. As the minutes ticked away, I could feel my heartbeat pick up. I was checking my watch every few seconds, tapping my side to make sure my gun was still there and looking at the sky for signs of the creatures' power source.

"Connell, calm down. It's going to be okay," Lilly said after watching me repeat the process a dozen more times.

I grinned at her and put my hands in my pockets. I continued to scan the crowds entering the zoo to see if I could find Jack and his crew. I was sure they had to be there somewhere. I wondered if Jack had a plan for my death yet and if he anticipated that I would be here. While I continued my visual search, I spotted someone I was not expecting. It was Melanie, who was a member of the group that hung out under the Chief's Head with Kevin and me. She was a nice girl, but socially awkward. She was with Tony, one of Jack's best friends. They were heading out of the zoo and towards the park.

"What is he doing with her?" I thought, starting to follow them.

"Connell, where are you going? The full moon is going to be up any moment," Andie Rae reminded me, grabbing my arm to stop me.

I continued to look towards Melanie until Andie Rae turned my head to face her.

"What's wrong?"

I pointed at them. "It's Melanie, she's with Tony, one of them. I can't let her just—"

Hayden interrupted me. "You can and you will."

I turned back to Hayden. Andie Rae stood between us.

"What … what are you saying?" I asked.

"She's not as important as the mission. I need you to focus."

I chose not to respond; instead, I looked one more time. Melanie disappeared into the park with Tony as Andie Rae led me back to our position.

Everyone started to shift their guns around under their trench coats. Hayden surveyed the sky in anticipation for what was about to unfold. Within seconds, the huge orb lit the sky up with its brilliance and I could feel the sweat begin to bead off my head.

"Remember, wait for the scream. Then unleash all your fury on them. I assure you they will do the same to you," Hayden said, staring into my eyes.

The seconds seemed like hours, and then we heard a loud, unique scream. However, it didn't come from the zoo. It came from the park.

I turned and took off running toward the park as fast as I could.

"*Pansy*, you get back here right now!" Hayden ordered, but I paid him no mind.

I ran through the parking lot, across the street, and into the park. I only stopped to pick up on the direction the moaning was coming from. After a few minutes following the noise, I came across them. Melanie was lying on her back, her torso torn apart, with Tony in his werewolf form standing over her, feeding on her flesh. The werewolf was black, with evil yellow eyes and long claws.

I ran from the tree line into plain sight and screamed at it. "Get away from her, you bastard."

The werewolf lifted his face from her body; it had blood smeared all across its snout. The creature began to snarl at me as it made its way across Melanie. I was petrified, but I wasn't going to leave her, not like that. I had to keep my composure together as it inched its way toward me. I slowly reached for my gun. The werewolf's demon-like eyes were following the movement of my hand. As I got closer to my weapon, it began to crouch down, preparing to lunge at me. It was too late to turn back now, and I knew, once I made my move, it was going to get really interesting around here. I swiftly pulled my gun from its holster. The creature leaped at me and was on top of me in seconds. It sank its teeth into me, knocking me to the ground; I dropped my gun. The beast was thrashing me around like a rag doll with its death grip on my shoulder. I was panicking, and the pain was beyond description. It tossed me about ten yards across the field, and I came to a sliding stop on my back. I grabbed my shoulder with my left arm, trying to stop the bleeding. As I attempted to sit up, the beast was back on top of me. It sank its massive fangs into my left arm and looked at me with those baleful yellow eyes. I screamed and stared back at it, wondering if this was the slow painful death Jack was telling me about. As the pressure increased on my arm, I could feel my bones cracking, but after what seemed like an eternity, my birthmark began to glow. It was as bright as the sun, and I could feel my muscular structure begin to mutate and contort my body. While I screamed in pain, my shirt tore apart, and the beast's mouth struggled to hold its grasp on my forearm. My blood felt like it was boiling, and my strength was unnatural. I grabbed the creature by its head with my free hand and pried it off me. I struck it as hard as I could with my bloody forearm and it stumbled back a few yards. I stood up and snarled at it while I flexed my new massive muscular structure.

All of my senses were focused on destroying the beast in front of me. I could hear it breathing and pawing the dirt, getting ready to lunge at me one more time. My reflexes were faster than a mongoose. As it made its feeble attempt to bite me, I grabbed its jaw with both hands and began to pull. I pulled as hard as I could as it struggled to free itself from my grasp. Its body was lashing in every direction to get away, but I was too powerful, too gigantic for it. I could feel its bones begin to separate in my hands and, just like that, the beast went limp. I dropped it to the ground and kicked it a few times to make sure it was dead. With no movement from it at all, I turned my attention to Melanie. She was clinging on to life, but I could see she was not going to be in this world much longer.

Dropping to my knees and still bleeding from the vicious attack, I picked her head up and gently put it in my lap. She looked up at me in agony.

"Mel, I'm so sorry," I said, stroking her head.

"Connell, I'm so cold. Help me, please," she pleaded as she struggled to breathe.

Tears streamed down my face. "Shhh, it's going to be okay, just rest. I'll stay with you."

She put her hand in mine, and after a few minutes she was gone. I remembered the talk at the shop about letting one go for the greater good. Somehow, it didn't seem worth it to me. I laid her head gently on the ground and tried to cover her torso the best I could with what remained of her clothing. I stood up and stared at her, feeling helpless. Then it hit me: Andie Rae.

I took off as fast as I could towards the zoo. As I got closer, I heard people screaming and the howls of the creatures paying tribute to the moon above. I crossed the street and saw the once beautiful white moon become overwhelmed with a deep red tint as I came to the outer wall of the zoo. The thought of that being because of Andie Rae made me panic. I scaled the wall of the zoo with little effort and landed in the manatee fountain inside the main entrance way. All around me was carnage, both man and beast. I could hear shots ringing out from multiple directions; Hayden, now in his wolf man form, was tearing creatures apart by the score. I frantically looked around for Andie Rae, but I couldn't find her. Lilly came limping towards the entrance and waved for me. I jumped out of the fountain and caught her as she collapsed into my arms. As I looked her over to make sure she wasn't bitten, she put her hand over my bloody shoulder.

"No, they got you!" she yelled in a panic.

I grabbed her hands as she thrashed around trying to get away from me.

"Lilly, calm down. I'm fine. Where's Andie Rae?"

She paused for a moment and, at last, realized I wasn't changing. She flung her arms around me, and held me tight, and started to cry. I removed her arms and put my hands on her cheeks.

I softly asked her, "Andie Rae ... where is she, Lilly?"

She attempted to calm herself down so she could communicate with me.

"She's back by the crocodile pit. There were too many of them. I tried to help, but she pushed me over the side so I could escape."

"Where's the croc pit?"

She pointed in the direction she came from. I let go of her face and took off running.

Along the way, I had to make the toughest decision of my life: stop to help people or sacrifice them to save her. I remembered what Doc had said back at the shop and how much I was against it. However, now that my personal interests were at stake, I found it a lot easier to think like the team, but it was for the wrong reasons. Was I a hypocrite? Maybe, but when I tried to save Melanie, it made no difference. She died just the same. Now I had the choice of saving total strangers that mean nothing to me or the girl I had waited for my entire life. I hardened my heart and ignored the screams of the victims. They looked so helpless and frightened, and I just stared back at them as I ran past. I was their last hope, and I ignored their needs for my own selfish wants. It was something I knew would come back to haunt me.

Turning a corner, I could hear gunshots. I was running so fast I was knocking people out of my way to get to her. Finally, after fearing the worst, I saw her. She was about twenty yards ahead of me, cornered and bloody. Thoughts raced through my mind—was I was too late? A dozen or so werewolves positioned themselves for the kill. The anger was so overpowering that any rational thought of my own safety was absent from my mind. I climbed the snack building next to me, hurried to the other side and leaped with all my might. I landed right in front of Andie Rae and was now the only thing standing between her and death. I let out a monstrous roar and charged the pack.

She screamed, "Connell, no!"

I couldn't think straight. The anger over Melanie and the fact that I'd almost lost Andie Rae clouded my better judgment. I bulldozed into the group, and they were all over me, biting and digging into my flesh. I screamed in pain and threw them off me as quickly as they attacked. Andie Rae crawled to the snack building where people inside opened the door and pulled her to safety.

I was overwhelmed by the numbers and lacked Hayden's experience. I couldn't continue to fight them off, so I did the only thing I could—I ran. Getting away from them turned out to be harder than I thought. I was weak from loss of blood, and they were determined to finish me off. I jumped off the decking into a field housing the zoo's grazing animals. Sensing the danger, they started to run away, and I knew my only hope for survival was to keep up with them. I ran toward the herd with the pack of creatures on my tail. Weaving in and out of the herd was the only way to avoid being bitten. I never thought to ask myself if I would be fast enough to keep up. There was just something inside me that knew I could. As we zigzagged through the prairie, the beasts snapped at me when they had an opportunity, but I was able to avoid them thanks to the mass confusion of the herd. I was becoming weaker, and these things were nowhere near ready to stop. They could smell my bloodied-up body, and it seemed like it was feeding their desire to finish me off. We approached a cliff, and there was only one thing I could do to survive.

I leaped off the cliff and spiraled down towards a body of water below. After plunging into the water, I was able to swim to shore and turn onto my back to make sure they weren't following me. I could see them up on the cliff staring down at me, snarling, and trying to decide what to do. After a few minutes, the leader of the pack let out an evil howl and led the beasts away from me. Exhausted, I could feel my body returning to its normal size. I had no energy to get up, so I lay there for hours, looking at a deep red moon and listening to people scream in agony.

Chapter Seven
A Change of Heart

I could feel her soft touch as she stroked my hair. Her scent was welcoming; I struggled to find the strength to open my eyes. I squeezed her hand tightly to tell her I knew she was there. She immediately laid her head on my chest, and I heard her let out a sigh of relief. When I attempted to maneuver into a more comfortable position, a searing sensation overtook my upper torso. My shoulder, and all the way down my arm, was very tender, and it was agonizing to move at all. I winced in pain and dropped back down on what I now realized was a bed.

"Where am I?" I asked, rubbing my eyes with my good hand.

"You're in Tampa General," a female voice answered.

Shocked, I moved back away from the girl who was comforting me and flinched in pain again.

"Lilly, is that you?" I asked, opening my eyes for the first time.

"Yes, it's me, and I'm so happy you're okay," she said, hugging me one more time.

I gently pushed her away—I was deeply confused. The last thing I remembered was looking up at the moon, and now, I was in a hospital bed with Lilly comforting me.

"How … how did I end up here? Where is Andie Rae?"

Lilly stood up from the bed and crossed her arms. It seemed I had offended her somehow, but I wasn't sure what I'd done.

"She took a break and went back to the shop to get some rest. She asked me to watch over you until she came back," she said curtly.

"Took a break? How long have I been here?"

"Three weeks. You lost a lot of blood, and the doctors were afraid you weren't going to make it."

I shook my head in disbelief and put my hand over my face.

"What? How is that possible? I was just lying on the bank staring at the moon."

Lilly returned to the side of my bed and sat down. She pulled my hand away from my face and turned my head to face her.

"Connell, we couldn't find you. We looked for you frantically until the police arrived and had the place surrounded. Hayden had to make the tough call to leave you—we had our weapons on us."

I snickered and rolled my eyes. "Tough call? There's no way I believe that."

"You're wrong, Connell! He *was* searching for you. He didn't want to leave, but Andie Rae talked him into it."

The shock of that statement was more than I could deal with at that moment. I rolled away from Lilly and asked her to leave.

"Connell, you don't understand."

I waved my hand to cut her off. I had no desire to hear what she had to say. "I understand all I need too. I want you to leave and tell your sister not to bother coming back up here."

Lilly paused for a moment, as if contemplating what she should say next. However, after a few seconds, I heard her stand up and leave the room without saying another word to me.

I was in the hospital for another forty-eight hours. The entire time I was angry at Andie Rae and the whole situation. I couldn't grasp the idea that I put my life on the line for her when she just left me to die. I felt like a fool, and I wanted to put everything behind me. I didn't ever want to return to the shop or see any of them again. All I wanted to do was to resume my dull life and make the most of it. It was clear that not only was the established hierarchy of high school a headache for me, but now I had to tiptoe around Chamberlain knowing that Jack and his creeps were looking to eliminate me.

The following Monday, I was at my subdivision entrance, waiting on that big yellow deathtrap. When it finally pulled up, the squeaky doors opened and the fat, disgusting bus driver was sitting there looking at me. I lowered my head and made my way towards the back of the bus. Plopping down into a seat, I winced and massaged my wounds. While my injuries had healed pretty well, the events at the zoo had left me in a lot of pain and with some ugly scars. Not only did I have to deal with my cursed birthmark, but I also had to deal with a constant reminder of Andie Rae. Life was now officially over for me. I thought it was bad already, but those last few of months, which had seemed so full of promise, had turned out to just to be another sad chapter in my miserable life. So much for being part of something new and exciting. At this rate, hanging out under the Chief's Head with the most socially incompetent people in the world sounded refreshing.

The bus pulled into Chamberlain, and, like clockwork, the pride of the pukes were eyeing which one of the kids they were going to bully today. I shook my head in disgust. Not only did those maggots go around feasting on whoever was unlucky enough to be where they were at full moon, they also felt the need to intimidate kids that didn't meet their standards. As we piled off the bus, Jack and his crew were waiting. Today, they picked out one of the nicest kids in the school, Xavier Green. He was easy prey for them: he was stout, dumpy, not the best-looking kid I knew, and one of the few African–American students at Chamberlain. It amazed me to watch every other outcast just run past him, only worried about their own welfare. It made me ill, and as I stepped off the bus, thoughts of Melanie raced through my mind. Was I going to just walk by and ignore this, or was I going to save him like I could have saved Mel? I knew this wasn't the best way to return to my old life, but not saving her and ignoring all those helpless people at the zoo to save someone who then left me for dead was eating away at me.

I dropped my backpack on a bench and took a deep breath. "You're a dolt, Maxwell," I whispered to myself.

As I approached them, I could hear Xavier beg for mercy. Jack was twisting his arm as hard as he could while his group laughed and cheered him on. I pushed my way through the crowd and shoved Jack away from Xavier with my good arm.

"Leave him alone, Jack," I demanded.

Jack got a hold of his footing and wiped his chest where I'd pushed him. He took his time walking back towards me. Typically, by now, this kind of episode would include Jack's buddies grabbing a hold of me, but they all seemed hesitant to do so. Jack and I were now nose to nose, and Xavier took the opportunity to scramble for the Chief's Head. Looking past Jack, I could see all the outcasts watching with interest as Xavier demonstrated the shove for them.

"Didn't you learn your lesson? Or does someone else have to disappear to get it through your thick head?"

"Well, Jack, if I count correctly, and I know it could be challenging for you and your buddies, I do believe we're all tied up right now."

Seeing that Jack and his cronies were absolutely clueless—they were all murmuring to each other, wondering what I meant—I softly said, "Tony."

They went silent and gazed at me with puzzled looks on their faces.

"What do you know about Tony?" Jack asked.

"I know that you shouldn't go wandering in the park during a full moon. It could be very dangerous for someone," I answered.

Now they all knew: they knew I was there. They knew I had something to do with Tony's not making it out of the park that night as planned. I could see the power drain out of their faces to be replaced with fear. The pride took a few steps back from me, babbling to themselves. Jack was more skeptical about what I was implying. He took a step in and punched me in the face. It was quick, hard, and accurate. I dropped to my knees immediately, and he began an assault on my ribs, kicking me over and over. As I crunched in pain, I could feel my birthmark starting to burn. I panicked, not knowing what my body was getting ready to do. I rolled away and plunged through the crowd and into the main entrance. Running down the hall, I crashed into the only person in Chamberlain High School worse than Jack: Mr. Farley.

"Mr. Maxwell, what is your malfunction today? Trying to plow over teachers now, are we?"

Looking down, holding my ribs, I simply apologized and said, "No, sir, I didn't see you there."

Mr. Farley, apparently realizing something was wrong, lifted my head up by my chin to see my bloody nose.

"So, it looks like karma finally caught up to you, Mr. Maxwell," he said with a chuckle.

Before I could answer, he took me by my arm to lead me to the nurse, exposing my birthmark, which was now bright red.

"Good grief, son, what are you doing to yourself?"

"Nothing," I quickly responded.

"This does not look like nothing to me, Mr. Maxwell," he said, and his demeanor shifted. "Quick, come in here."

He led me into his classroom and had me sit in a chair next to his desk. He went to his closet and pulled out the first aid kit. There was an awkward silence, but Mr. Farley took care of me. He wiped my nose clean, wrapped my birthmark, which was fading now, and offered me some Tylenol for my ribs. He took his seat and stared at me for a few minutes. I stared out the window—I was totally out of my comfort zone with the way he was acting towards me.

Leaning forward, he dropped his pen on his desk, started to rub his head and said, "Mr. Maxwell, I am sorry."

"Excuse me, Mr. Farley?" I countered in disbelief, turning towards him.

"Don't be funny, son, I'm being serious. I'm sorry I did not take notice about how rough you've had it here at Chamberlain. These wounds explain a lot to me. Who did this to you?"

I was not sure I wanted to tell him, but I was mesmerized by this olive branch. The answer just slipped out. "Jack Alexander and his crew."

"I see. Do they do it often?" he asked, leaning back in his chair.

"Every day to multiple people," I answered.

"Very well. I will handle this. And you should expect no further issues out of that group, or they will have me to deal with. However, I need something from you in exchange."

"What is that?" I asked.

"I need you to trust me and come talk to me. Regardless of our past, I am here for you and all my students."

I was not sure what to make of this. Everything in my life was so upside down, and now the man who had nothing but disdain for me wanted me to trust him and come to him with all of my problems.

"Sure, I guess," I muttered.

"What was that?" he asked, leaning forward in his chair with both hands clasped

I let out a deep sigh and said, "Yes, sir."

"Good, Mr. Maxwell, very good." He pulled out a piece of paper and started to write on it.

"Here is my phone number. If you have any issues at all, and I mean *any* issues, you just give me a buzz, and I'll be quick to handle it." He smiled as he handed me the note.

I leaned back in my chair and shoved the note deep into my front pocket. This had to be the last thing on earth I ever expected to happen between me and Mr. Farley. However, right now, with no friends and a whole bunch of enemies, I figured it wouldn't hurt.

Mr. Farley spent a few more minutes cleaning me up, and, when the bell rang, Mrs. Perry walked in. She seemed very upset and out of character.

"Mr. Farley, I need a word with you, please."

"Of course, Mrs. Perry. Mr. Maxwell, will you excuse us?"

I grabbed my belongings and left without saying a word. Behind the closed door, I could hear them arguing back and forth. While I would have loved to know what was going on, the last thing I needed to do was get caught eavesdropping, so I headed out to the Chief's Head. I was in no mood to attend class—after all, the one teacher that made the day the most interesting had just become my confidant. How in the heck did that happen? I mean, our rivalry was one for the ages, and, just like that, it was taken from me. Unfortunately, that seemed like the current theme to my pathetic life.

While I was slouching on the red benches under the watchful eye of the all-knowing Chief, Xavier appeared from around the corner reading the latest role-playing book that many of the outcasts spend every minute of their lives obsessing over. He plopped down beside me, put his custom wand placeholder in his book, and stared at me with the most annoying grin.

"What?" I said after a few awkward moments of silence.

"Hey, Connell, how are you doing?" he asked, searching for something in his bag.

"Well, let's see, Xavier—I got my tail kicked this morning, I am bruised, in pain, and I had to spend about twenty minutes with Mr. Farley. So, how would you say I'm doing?" I asked sarcastically.

"Oh, well, about that. I wanted to thank you for helping me out. I never had anyone stand up for me before. It was nice to know that someone, anyone cares." His eyes started to water while he continued his search.

Those comments really caught me off guard. They were the same as Kevin had said to me on the first day of school when I took a beating for him. Here I was feeling sorry for myself for never being part of the group that Xavier and the rest of the outcasts feared. I started to wonder if I was just as bad as those who picked on them every day because I consistently tried to separate myself from some of the most caring, friendly, and appreciative people I knew. I felt horrible; while I never physically harmed any of the outcasts. I certainly verbally assaulted them on a regular basis. What kind of piece of crap did that make me? How could I not see this before? I was the very thing I hated, and it made me sick.

"Don't worry about it. It was the right thing to do," I finally responded.

"Yes, I found it," Xavier said, pulling out a piece of paper from his bag.

Turning towards me, he handed me a mustard-stained invitation to his monthly role-playing game after school under the bleachers of the football stadium.

"It would be so cool if you could come. Our group is always looking for more players, and we bring pizza with soda."

I could see the sweat begin to bead on his forehead. Rejection was commonplace for him and his crew, but he was hopeful which made him nervous. I looked down at the piece of paper and pretended like I was actually interested, nodding my head as I read it over. It was a bunch of nonsense, the kind of stuff Kevin used to always read to me and be into.

I sighed and said, "Sure, Xavier, I would love to check it out."

He wiped his brow and started to chuckle. "Really, you would?"

"*Yes*, Xavier, I would love to," I said, even though I really did not mean it.

"Great, so just to let you know, all of the guys go by their playing names, so be thinking of what name you would like to go by."

"I'll think long and hard on that one, Xavier," I said in a semi-mocking tone.

"Yeah, I'll see you at the gathering, Connell." He collected his things, still smiling from ear to ear.

As he started to walk away, I said to him, "So, Xavier, what name do you go by?"

He paused and looked down at the floor, turning to me with a very serious look and whispered, "They call me the Beast Slayer."

Nodding my head in approval, I roared, "See you later, Beast Slayer."

He bowed to me and replied, "My pleasure, kind sir."

I could not help but laugh inside as he walked away. He was so genuine, kind, and friendly. Perhaps I'd had this all wrong my entire life. Maybe being popular was not really the important thing or something I should be putting all my energy towards. Perhaps just being a good, kind person, which Xavier mastered in spades, was all anyone truly needed in life. Why had I missed this?

Again, I found myself wondering who made these sucky rules in life. What made punks the popular bunch and the kind, quiet ones on the outside looking in? There had to be some kind of special punishment that person was going through right now. Maybe his or her punishment was realizing what I knew now and it being too late to do anything about it. Being an outcast or different is not a burden or a curse. It's about setting standards for yourself and never wavering from who you are. It's about being you and loving yourself to do just that.

I got up and decided to head to class; after all, what was really that terrible in my life? The only thing I could think of was that I could not share this revelation with Kevin. He was one of them, and I just never wanted to admit it to myself. I opened the main door to the school, and as I slowly strolled down the hall, it hit me: there should not be *us* or *them*, just *we*. How did I screw that up? I wiped a tear from my eye that bubbled up from the shame of who I'd become and made a vow to myself not to judge people who did not fit into a certain box. I needed to try to understand and be a friend to them.

I found myself thinking I may even have fun hanging out with Xavier and the rest of the outcasts. I was even thinking about the guys at the shop. After all, they were their own type of outcast, and they all had each other. I wasn't sure I wanted to go back and get involved or even if they would have me back. For that matter, I was not even sure I wanted to continue to explore what destiny they felt I was supposed to accomplish. I just needed to come up with a cool name for myself if I was going to hang out with the outcasts and hope I was smart enough to keep up with all that stuff Kevin used to live and breathe. Boy, I wished I could talk to him about it instead of telling him to shut up. I opened the door to English class. I needed to concentrate so that I didn't fall asleep in the next forty-five minutes.

Chapter 8
Filtiarn

The day had finally arrived. It was time for me to meet under the football bleachers with Xavier and the rest of the outcasts who participated in their monthly event. I was on edge, not only because I wasn't sure how I'd fit in, but it was also the first full moon since I stopped talking to the gang at the shop. I couldn't help but feel worried about them, especially Andie Rae. The last two times out, she'd needed me, and I felt I was letting her down in some way. That line of thinking was crazy, though, since she basically abandoned me at the zoo. Still, there was something that didn't allow me to hang on to that anger; instead, it increasingly changed to fear. Not only for her, but for Lilly and the rest of the gang at the shop. I even paused every now and again and thought about Hayden, but in a different way. It was clear that he could handle himself in those situations, but I always felt he put the mission before people, and it may end up one day killing someone or everyone at the shop.

When the bell rang to end class, I started to walk towards the stadium. It was the end of the football team's season, and, as usual, the mighty Chiefs made the playoffs and were starting practice for their game against Plant High School. As I walked down the one hundred hall of Chamberlain, Mr. Farley emerged from his room with his briefcase and the keys to his car.

"Mr. Maxwell, a word with you please?" he asked.

I made my way over to him, putting my hands in my pockets and letting out a small sigh. He had been overly friendly to me in the last few days and had even stepped in, unleashing the wrath that used to be reserved for me on Jack and his cronies. I never realized how much I enjoyed my rivalry with Mr. Farley until it was gone. Mr. Farley kind of filled that void by being kinder and supportive, but I found it dull at best. I still was expecting things to return to normal with him, but, for now, he was providing the break that the outcasts and I could only dream of. There hadn't been a single attack since we talked.

"Hey, Mr. Farley, what's up?" I said.

"Where are you heading?" he asked.

Looking around to see who was nearby, I mumbled, "I'm heading to the stadium to meet up with a group of friends to participate in their club."

"Ahh, the role-playing club put on by Mr. Green. Well, good for you. They're a smart group of kids—you'll like them very much." He signaled me to walk with him.

We walked towards the stadium, and he asked me if I was having any problems with Jack and his group. When I acknowledged that it has been extremely quiet and thanked him for his help, he patted me on the back and assured me it was the least he could do. We continued to chat about school, grades, my plans for the future, and how I was doing with the Kevin situation. It was nice to have someone to talk with, even if I couldn't tell him everything. Why bother—it wasn't like he would believe me anyway. He would properly have me locked up or something. Approaching the football stadium, I could see Jack and his boys hanging around the gym entrance. They completely ignored us as we passed them by. I shook my head in amazement and smirked. This was actually working—I was free to return to my life, and it was all thanks to Mr. Farley. That just sounded weird to me. When we cleared the gym, I could see Xavier and about three other kids sitting under the stadium waiting for me.

I turned to Mr. Farley and said, "Thanks for the talk, Mr. Farley, it means a lot."

"Any time, Mr. Maxwell," he responded, putting his hand on my shoulder.

He turned around and walked back towards the gym, where Jack and his group bumped into him. They were not paying attention; they were all reading a paper Jack had in his hand. Mr. Farley was not pleased, and I couldn't help but smile as he tore into them for being incompetent athletes. He snatched the piece of paper out of Jack's hand, crumpled it up, and threw it away in the trash can. He continued to yell at them for a few more minutes and then ordered them to run to the locker room. After they were out of sight, Mr. Farley brushed off his shirt and walked away mumbling under his breath, shaking his head, and blushing.

I used the opportunity while the no one was looking to run over to the trash can and pull out the crumpled piece of paper. I unraveled it quickly to see what those morons were planning. To my disappointment, it only had an address, some directions, and a date on it. From the directions, I knew it was near the park with the giant strawberry tower in Plant City. Outside of that, I had no idea what the significance of the location was. However, I could tell by the date that it would fall during next month's full moon. I was torn; should I go back to the shop and give this information to the gang, or should I ignore it and continue living my life?

"Hey, Connell, come on, we're ready to start the meeting," Xavier said, waving his arms in my direction.

"Yeah, I'm coming," I said, shoving the note in my pocket to deal with later.

I made my way over to the group and greeted Xavier. He corrected me immediately and reminded me that during these meetings he was only to be called the Beast Slayer. I nodded my head in agreement and took in the personalities of the people he introduced. Greta Chow, otherwise known as Vandree during the meetings, was one of the smartest people in the entire school. She was very pretty, but she wore thick glasses that made her eyes look like she had fish bowls over them. Santiago Fernandez, also known as Zyn, was the child of Cuban immigrants who had recently made the dangerous voyage to the United States. Because he understood limited English, he had trouble fitting in. His trademark was a constant smile and nodding in agreement no matter what was said. Finally, there was Prisha Patel, also known as Maya. Prisha was the only Indian in the school. She was kind of an enigma to me—I knew her parents enforced a lot of rules, and her ability to engage at school was very limited. If she was not studying or doing homework, she was required to work at her family's restaurant, Satir. I wondered if she actually had permission to participate in this group or if she was going behind her parents' backs.

"Hey, guys, it's nice to meet you. I'm Connell."

"It's very nice to meet you, Connell. Would you like some pizza?" Greta asked.

"Sure, that would be awesome."

The pizza was perfect. It was New York Style with large chunks of pepperoni and sausage. When you picked it up, you had to fold it in half because the slices were so large. But the best part was the grease that flowed down when you tilted the slice. Those were all hallmarks of really good pizza. I savored every bit, and we continued to make small talk, trying to get to know each other.

"So, what's the deal with the birthmark?" Xavier asked.

I choked on my pizza and patted my chest a few times, then asked, "How do you know about that?"

"Kevin told us about it when he came to the meetings," Prisha said.

I started to wonder how many people Kevin had told without me knowing. Was I wasting my time wearing long-sleeved shirts? With all those questions racing through my head, for the first time I wasn't upset about it. I couldn't be. My friend, who I would have been all over for this, was not here, and I still missed him very much. So I did the very thing Kevin would have wanted: I rolled up my sleeve and showed them.

"That is incredible," Xavier proclaimed, clutching my arm to fully extend it.

Rubbing my birthmark, Greta said, "It's in perfect condition and proportionate."

"*Si, sin duda es la marca del* wolf man," Santiago added.

"What did he say?" I asked the group.

"He basically said it is the mark of the wolf man," Prisha said.

"So, you all believe in that stuff?" I probed.

"Come on, Connell, all those attacks across town—do you really think wild beasts get out of the zoo that often?" Greta asked sarcastically.

"That stuff may fool the people of this town, but for pros like us, we've been tracking this story for months," Xavier said.

"Why do you all care so much?" I asked.

"Because when the time comes, we want to be ready to defend ourselves," Prisha answered.

I chuckled. "The ones who run off the bus and make a dash for the Chief's Head, you all are going to defend yourselves against beasts?"

"Well, we are at least planning on how we would handle the situation. That's the main theme of our gaming. What would we do in case of an attack? It fits perfectly in our world." Greta pulled out a large notebook. She handed it to me. It was filled with scenarios I had been part of and others that ranged from a school attack to the local grocery store. The guys each had a role and tactics with identified weapons that they would use in each scenario. I continued to flip through the notebook and accidentally exposed some of the scars on my arm from the fight with Tony.

Grabbing my arm and pulling up my sleeve, Santiago shouted, "*¿Que te paso?*"

Understanding what he said, Greta pulled my arm away from him and said, "He wants to know what the happened to you, and so do I."

I pulled my arm back and lied. "It was just a bite from a dog I used to have, guys."

"What kind of dog did your parents allow you to have?" Xavier asked.

"It was my grandmother's dog. I've lived with her since my parents died in a car accident a few years ago. She's not all there, but she tries her best," I answered, clasping my hands and looking down.

"I am so sorry, I had no idea, Connell," Xavier answered.

"Dude, don't worry about it—it's not like you could have known."

Putting his hand on my shoulder, Santiago quietly said, "*Tambien he perdido a muchos parientes en Cuba. Asi que se como te sientes.*"

"He said, he has lost many relatives back in Cuba, so he understands how you feel," Greta said as she lifted her thick glasses to wipe the tears under them.

I simply nodded at him and said, "Thanks."

Santiago gave me that all-too-familiar smile, stood up, went back over to where the pizza was, and grabbed another slice. The others, clearly not really knowing what to say, started to pull role-playing books out of their backpacks and explained the rules of the club, the games, and how they carried out their missions.

After about a half hour, I felt overwhelmed with the specifics that were provided, yet many of their assumptions and thought processes when it came to werewolves were very accurate. As far as the other things such as Trolls, Orks, and Wizards, well, I just rolled with it. We started to wrap things up, and Xavier forwarded me the meeting invite on my phone. When I stood and began to pack up, I realized we had forgotten to give me a name.

Turning around to the guys, I asked, "So when do I get my name?"

"Man, we almost forgot that. What have you come up with?" Xavier asked.

"To be honest, I didn't. I have no idea about this stuff and what names are good and what names suck."

The guys huddled around and started to debate quietly so that I couldn't overhear them. There were some very passionate conversations going on, based on the body language they were using.

In the end, they must have all really liked the name because Santiago was smiling and clapping loudly when they broke the huddle.

"So, what is it?" I asked.

"After much debate, we have decided it will be, Filtiarn," Xavier said.

"Filtiarn? What the heck is that?"

"Based on your mark, we think it's the perfect name. It means lord of the wolves," Greta replied.

Smirking and nodding, I concluded that was one heck of a fitting name. "Okay … Filtiarn it is," I said as I picked up my bag. "Well, guys, it's been more fun than I thought it would be, thanks for inviting me. I'll see you all later."

They said their goodbyes, and I started to walk home. This gang was different from the others at Horror and Things, but in a good way. They were all sane, not looking to get anyone killed, and they were having fun. Part of me wished the others could see what life was meant to be and how much they were missing out on. But I knew they had acclimated to the life they led. I found myself on the fence; I had finally found a group of people I fit in with, but, at the same time, I knew the truth. I knew what was lurking out there, I knew what was going to happen tonight, and I knew that the guys would put their lives on the line again for all of us. Was it fair of me to ignore what I knew and what I had been able to do to help them? Would it be my fault that people would die in the future since I supposedly had the power to stop all this? I reached into my pocket and pulled out the note.

While I was reading it, I wandered into the parking lot where Jack and his maggots were all gathered out after practice. The strange thing was that Mrs. Perry was hanging out with them. They were all laughing and cutting up like they were best buds or something. It could have been she was just trying to connect to her students, but I was not confident in that anymore. I hung back and watched her being chummy with the very people she defended us against during school hours, and it made me sick to my stomach. As I froze in place in my disbelief, she turned and saw me, changing her demeanor on a dime back to what we had all come to expect from her. She pointed out some issues with the cars' parking passes and quickly excused herself. I watched her walk quickly back to the school and disappear through the main entrance. Puzzled, I looked back to see Jack and the gang peel out of the parking lot, heading away from the school. I looked down at the note one more time, hopeful that the sloppily written address would provide me some answers.

Chapter 9
Payback

First thing in the morning, I jumped out of bed, turned on the news channel and surfed the web to see if there were any attacks last night. I was sickened to discover that twenty people had been killed throughout the city by so-called wild dogs, but I couldn't find anything that supported a central location. I leaned back in my chair and sighed deeply. Perhaps Hayden hadn't been able to find out where the meet was going to be held. I welcomed that thought; I knew it meant that the others would be safe. Looking at my desk, I remembered the piece of paper Jack and his cronies had been yapping over. I picked it up and read it again. Still with no clue about what it meant, I fell back on to my bed and rubbed my chin. I had to make a difficult choice: did I go back down to Horror and Things and give this information to the guys or did I just forget about it? I went back and forth as I got ready for school, and, with each decision I made, I was committed to it for at least a minute. When I was ready to go out, still undecided on which route to take, I snatched the piece of paper from my desk and shoved it in my pocket.

Waiting for the bus to arrive with its obese, hairless sap of a driver, I thought about the piece of paper and what I should do. If I gave it to the group, I would be saving lives and perhaps get back in good standing; if I didn't, I would be saying goodbye to them and

Andie Rae forever. I propped myself against a tree and ran my hands through my hair in frustration. The big yellow casket of death was approaching, and I could see the driver's grin. I shook my head and boarded the bus without making eye contact. I made my way to my seat and dropped down next to Xavier.

"Hey, man, how's it going?" he asked as he finished his math assignment.

Taking off my backpack and dropping it between my legs, I answered, "It's going—I mean we're going to school, right, so how good could it be?"

Xavier stopped and stared at me. "Man, I wasn't talking about school, I was talking about that," he said pointing at my arm.

"Come on, Xavier, you know that's a bunch of nonsense," I snapped back cynically.

He turned back to his textbook and simply said, "Whatever you say, dude."

"What is that supposed to mean?" I asked.

"I just thought you and I were going to be tight, but if you don't want to open up to me, I can't force you to," Xavier said, turning the page in his math book.

I thought about it for a second and responded the only way I could at the moment. "Look, I know you're a smart guy and I do trust you, but I need to just figure me out first. Just give it time."

He looked up and smirked at me. "Connell, take all the time you need. I just hope you know I'll be there if you need me," he said, packing up his bags as we pulled into Chamberlain.

"Thanks dude, I appreciate you getting it."

I surveyed the lot for the pride of pukes. With none of Jack's group in sight, I picked up my backpack, confused. Every day, they were here without fail to pick on someone and today—nothing. As we piled off the bus, I felt a sense of relief from the crowd as they leisurely made their way towards the Chief's Head. I continued to look in every direction, waiting for an ambush, but it never came. Taking a seat under the mighty Chief, we could see the entire parking lot, and to my delight, it was very empty today. The spot where Jack and his crew hung out had zero cars around it. The rest of the outcasts were as perplexed as I was. There was a lot of murmuring amongst the crowd, some of them pointing to the spot the pride called home.

"What do you think is going on?" asked Xavier.

"Not sure, but I don't like it at all," I answered, continuing to scan the area.

"¿Hey, *chicos, donde estan los matones este* morning?" Santiago asked, joining the group with Greta and Prisha in tow.

"He wants to know where the bullies are," Greta translated, slumping down onto a bench.

"What's wrong with you?" Xavier asked.

"We just passed Mrs. Perry in the hall, and she was talking with the principal, Ms. Whitehead, about the plans for the winter bonfire," Greta said.

"What's so bad about the bonfire?" Prisha asked. She was never allowed to attend.

"It's when all the popular kids are celebrated for their athletic achievements while we sit bored out of our minds, listening to the in-crowd become tighter while everyone else is shoved further out," Xavier said, pushing me by the shoulder to fall away from him to demonstrate his point.

"On top of that, once it's done we all go into the gym for a celebration. One where we all sit on the bleachers and watch the popular kids have fun. Sometimes I feel like the system is set up to work against us," Greta continued.

"That has to be the biggest waste of time for the majority of the school. Why do they make us all go to it?" I said, kicking a rock into the grass.

"Because, dude, Ms. Whitehead thinks that we need to be supportive of Chamberlain, and how can we do that if we're not there?" Xavier reasoned, shrugging his shoulders in disgust.

"*Hombre, eso es una mierda,*" Santiago shouted, crossing his arms in front of him.

"You're right about that Santiago, that does suck," Greta confirmed.

"Any way we can get out of it?" I asked the group.

"Only if you're willing to give up five percent of your grade in each class or have a parents' excuse. That's how serious she is about it," Prisha answered.

The first bell rang.

"No point in being anxious about that now, we have plenty of time before the bonfire for dread, fear, and intimidation," Xavier said, standing up.

"True enough. I'll see you all at lunch." I picked up my bag and headed towards the gym.

I know teachers and the principals are not blind to our struggles. It just amazes me that they always talk about inclusion and school being a safe place, but their actions promote the segregation we experience every day. The reality that they hold up these athletes as the school darlings, knowing that a lot of them terrorize us each day, just sucks. They know the athletes make the social rules of the school, but I wish, for once, they would look at it from our eyes rather than just do what they think is best.

"Connell, a word please," a female voice called out behind me.

"Oh, hey, Mrs. Perry," I said turning around, shocked to see her approaching me.

"Where are you heading?"

"To gym class," I answered.

"Do you mind if I tag along?"

"No, not at all," I lied.

We leisurely made our way towards the gym, and instead of interrogating me some more, she reverted back to being a woman with a caring ear who wanted to be there for the outcasts. She asked me how my grandmother was and how I was doing without Kevin. I gave her short simple answers because I was really confused. Was she buddying up to me because I saw her with Jack or did she really mean it? It seemed like Mr. Farley and her were having out-of-body experiences or something with their constant personality changes lately.

"Well, here we are. I hope you have a wonderful day, and if you need anything, please come see me," she said.

"Thanks Mrs. Perry, I appreciate it," I responded.

With Mrs. Perry now out of sight, I walked up to the main entrance of the gym and found a sign instructing us to go to the side doors. I took the steps down to the side and under the home football stands. It was really quiet over there, with Jack and his gang nowhere in sight. The weight room was here and so was the football locker room. Those two places were the equivalent of the Chief's Head to that gang. Just as they don't come under the Head so they're not linked to our group, we avoid this area during the school day out of fear. I pulled on the large red metal door and walked into the boys' locker room. It was dark and dreary as always. Making my way towards my locker, I could hear some whispering coming from the shower room and wondered why everyone was in there. I turned the corner to investigate and I found all the outcasts in my class corralled by some of Jack's group. I knew immediately it was a trap, so I turned and ran as fast as I could to the exit doors. When I flung them open I realized what I suspected: it was too late.

Jack and a bunch of his friends were waiting on me. I was surrounded and had no way of escaping. They forced me back into the middle of the locker room, leaving a few people in the shower room to keep the nerds in there, and posted two others at the doors to watch out for staff members. Judging by the size of the crowd, I was about to get the biggest beat down in the history of Chamberlain High School.

"Time for retribution, Maxwell," Jack said, herding me closer to the lockers.

I did the only thing I could think of in that moment. I made a joke at Jack's expense. "I think you have the wrong guy. I think you're looking for your dad for having you," I said, smirking.

The beating was fast and furious. The punches and kicks came like flashes of lightning, rhythmically and from all directions. I could feel the blood trickle down my face, and my gut was tight and pulsating with pain. The blows felt like they would go on forever—I felt my body go limp. After I fell to the ground, I could feel someone's shoe across my throat. I gagged in pain while reaching up to try and lift the muscle-bound leg off me, to no avail.

"This is just a sample of what's waiting for you, Maxwell," Jack said, keeping up the pressure on my throat. "First Tony, then that crazy redneck you bring to the school, and finally ratting us out to Mr. Farley. Do you actually think any of that will make a difference?"

I struggled to say anything, but I got a few words out: "Go fly a kite, Jack."

In a fury, Jack had a couple of his friends pick me up and hold me while he assaulted my ribs some more. I tried to control my temper during the entire ordeal. The last thing I needed was for my birthmark to act up in school. I could feel the burning sensation over the immense pain, but I would not allow myself to give in to it. After a few more blows, they shoved me in a locker and slammed it shut on me.

"Next time, Maxwell, we're going to finish the job," Jack said, signaling his guys to retreat into the gym.

I listened as their footsteps became faint. I could hear the guys from the showers make their way into the main locker room, talking amongst themselves, wondering what happened. They were strict rule followers, and they departed for the gym hastily so that they would not be tardy. I opened the locker and wiped my face with my forearm to clear some off the blood as I stepped out. Grabbing my ribs in pain, I made my way over to one of the sinks and attempted to clean myself up as much as I could before leaving the locker room. I needed to avoid Jack and his gang until I could get my bearings, so I headed back to the Chief's Head, knowing I would be safe there.

As the minutes slowly ticked away, I sat and stared at the cars zipping by the parking lot. The hardest part of that beating was that I knew I could have stopped it if I had only allowed my anger to go unchecked. But how in the world would have I been able to explain that to anyone? The longer I sat there, the more depressed I got. It seemed that the more I tried to fit in with anyone, the more trouble it brought. The thought that Mr. Farley could actually help in this situation was laughable. I couldn't believe I was that big a fool. Rules are rules and in the end the popular kids always have a way to come out on top. The more I moved, the more it hurt, but I didn't care. I was just so sick and tired of this game, and there was only one way I knew how to end it.

"Mr. Maxwell, what are you doing out here?" Mr. Farley asked, coming around the corner. "You're tardy to class … what happened?" He took a seat next to me and looked at my bruised face.

"Nothing, Mr. Farley. I'll be okay," I said, still staring at the traffic.

"Now, son, how can I help you—?"

"You can't!" I shouted, interrupting him. "I appreciate all you tried to do, but the rules don't work that way."

"Rules, what rules?"

"You know—the rules that every school-aged kid lives with. There are the popular ones who get everything, and then the rest of us. The bullies and the bullied. The strong and the weak."

"Why don't we go back to my office and chat some more?" he asked, seeing other outcasts starting to make their way to the Chief's Head for lunch.

I stood up and grabbed my stuff. "Sorry, Mr. Farley, you can't help me with this one. I have to handle it on my own." I started to walk away towards the parking lot.

"Mr. Maxwell, where are you going? Mr. Maxwell," he shouted.

I did not respond or look back towards him. I wanted to get as far away from that place as I could before Xavier and the gang saw me. I didn't want them to get wrapped up in this mess, and I knew they would have all types of questions for me. I cared too much about them, and I wasn't going to lose them the way I lost Kevin. For their safety, I figured it would be best for me to keep a low profile until I could figure this all out. I was all alone, which made me vulnerable. I had no idea what I was going to do next, but I knew I needed to figure it out, and quick, because the next time Jack caught up with me, the outcome may be a lot worse than today's.

Chapter 10
Redemption

For the next three weeks, instead of going to school, I would jump on the bus and head down to Ybor City each day trying to work up the courage to walk into Horror and Things. Typically, I found myself across the street, sitting on the roof of a restaurant and watching the gang go in and out of the shop. Lilly was starting to grow her hair out, and Andie Rae had introduced some blue to her pink highlights. It always made me feel warm inside to see those two, especially Andie Rae. I wondered if she would ever talk to me again after the hospital stunt. More than that, I wondered if Hayden would allow me to walk out of the shop alive if I ever had the fortitude to go over there.

Each day was the same: they went in and out of the shop in pairs, smiling and carrying on like they had no cares in the world. Well, everyone except Hayden, of course. That dude always had some type of chip on his shoulder and was never shy about showing it. The UPS truck pulled up once or twice daily, dropping off crates I was positive had nothing to do with merchandise for the shop, but contained equipment more appropriate for killing werewolves. I laughed each time Bear pushed Toby and Doc aside to carry a case they were struggling with. I knew Bear meant nothing by it and would do anything for those two. I was sure he just wanted to get it done so he could move on to something he enjoyed, like eating.

It was the day before the next full moon and I still hadn't worked up enough nerve to go into the shop. I'd missed so much school that I had no idea how I was going to catch up on my work. I had to intercept a few notes that were intended for my grandmother from Mrs. Perry and Mr. Farley. I was an expert at forging her signature and I simply sent back something to both of them stating that I was ill and would provide a doctor's note when I returned. I hated taking advantage of her like that, but even if I showed her the notes, she wouldn't remember them a few hours afterwards. So why upset her? She had already been through so much, and I knew she didn't have a lot of time left. I tried to make life for her as stress-free as possible and kept my problems to myself.

I'd been sitting on the roof for a few hours, and I hadn't seen any movement in or out of Horror and Things. The UPS driver had just delivered his first crate of the day, but it just sat outside the main doors. Wondering where the guys were, I decided to go down and check out the crate for myself. I carefully descended the fire escape, looking all round for anyone from the gang. With the area clear, I sprinted across the street and went to inspect the crate. It was smaller than the others but very heavy, and completely nailed shut. I had a look at the label to see where it came from. It was hard to read as it was torn; however, I thought it was from Triggers Gun Shop out in Mills, Wyoming. I pulled out my phone to look the dealer up, and to no surprise, it was a small mom-and-pop dealer in the middle of nowhere. It was a genius move; a small operation out west would not raise too many questions about the shipment. I scrolled down to see what other information I could find on the owners, but I came up disappointed. After spending more time than I wanted out there on the street, I turned to head back to the roof.

"Care to explain to me what you're doing?" a voice asked.

"Oh snap—you scared the crap out of me!" I jumped back from the crate. "What are you doing here, Xavier?"

"I knew you've been missing classes a lot, and from my conversations with Kevin, I figured you would be here."

Looking around, I grabbed him by the arm and led him back across the street. "Come on, we need to move before they get back."

"Are you going to tell me what's going on?"

"*Yes*—just come on!" I pulled harder.

After scurrying across the street and making our way back to the rooftop, we both sat down with the shop in clear view. I saw Bear's truck pull up. Hayden was in the passenger seat with Toby and Doc in the bed. Following close behind them were Andie Rae and Lilly in the car we took up to Bear's house.

"Look, they're back," I said, crouching down. I made my way to the edge to get a better view.

"Who's back?" Xavier asked, following me.

"The guys from Horror and Things."

"Connell, none of this is making a lick of sense, can you help me understand?"

I sighed and decided to tell him some of the details about my encounters with the guys. I left it very vague to protect Xavier and to squash any desire he may have to join Hayden's escapades. What I said mostly revolved around Andie Rae, our weekend together, and how wonderful it was. I told him that I felt like I'd been given a once in a lifetime opportunity, and I screwed my chance with her up.

After listening to me babble for a while, he interrupted me. "What are you waiting for then? Go down there and see her."

"What if she rejects me?"

"Well, man, you can either watch life go by and protect yourself, or you can take a risk along the way and see what happens."

I chuckled and asked, "Where did you get that from?"

Xavier put his hand on my shoulder and said, "From you, that day you put your neck on the line for me back at Chamberlain." Standing up he continued. "You took a big risk for me, not knowing how it would turn out, and I hope you feel it was worth it."

I sat down again and stared ahead at the shop, nodding in agreement. "Thanks, Xavier."

"Anytime, my man. I have to get going. I'll see you later?"

I looked up at him and nodded. "For sure."

After watching Xavier make his way down the fire escape, I turned my attention back to the shop. He was right—it was time for me to stopping messing around with this and take a risk. If it paid off, a lot of people could be saved in addition to me getting back in with the group. If not, I would have tried my best to do what was right, and, hopefully, I'd get to walk out of there in one piece. I started to make my way towards the shop, and I could feel my heart racing. Beads of sweat were forming on my forehead and neck like an army ready to be unleashed.

With each step, my hands shook a little more and the sweat was now like waves crashing over the bridge of my nose. I stood outside, wiped my face one last time, and then opened the door. Stepping in and shutting it behind me, I could feel the stares. I slowly turned around; they were all there except for Bear and Hayden. I surveyed each one of them. Doc and Toby had puzzled looks on their faces, like you have when you wonder what the heck someone's thinking. Lilly had a huge smile on her face, which put me a little at ease. As for Andie Rae, I could tell she was really upset with me; however, I had no way of knowing how much. I approached the bar where they all were, and before I could say anything, I heard a loud friendly roar as Bear entered the room.

"Well, look at what we have here—you decided to come on home. You're dead as disco when Hayden gets here, son. You know he didn't take too kindly to you scattering on us," he said, taking a seat on the bar facing me. "I'm as anxious as a one-eyed cat watchin' two rat holes," he concluded, rubbing his calloused hands together.

"That's enough, Bear," Doc yelled across the bar. He walked around the counter and shook my hand. "Welcome home, Connell,

I'm happy to see you. I don't understand why you're here, but I'm happy you are."

"What about Hayden?" Toby asked, frantically cleaning his glasses.

"What about him?" Doc said, turning back towards the guys. "Sure, he'll be upset, but he has always put the mission above his personal feelings, and I don't see why he wouldn't do that here."

Doubting Doc, Bear cocked his head with a sarcastic smile and responded, "Well, Doc, he ain't going to be as happy as a 'coon in the cornfield with all the dogs tied."

"Yes, Bear, he will be angry, but come on, how many times has he been mad at you and got over it?" Lilly asked.

"That's true, sugar." He got up and put his hefty arm around me. "I've been in the dog house with Hayden so many times that when I meet another man, I don't know whether to shake his hand or sniff his tail."

Toby just nodded in agreement as he continued to wipe his already cleaned glasses. Doc shook his head and walked away from Bear. Andie Rae kept silent and glared at me. Lilly and I cracked up laughing, which seemed to make Bear's day.

Bear grabbed me by the face with his other monstrous hand and planted a kiss on my cheek before returning to his stool. Andie Rae, still apparently emotionless, walked straight up to me and slapped me across the other cheek.

"How dare you," she shouted, slapping me a few more times.

I grabbed her hand to stop the onslaught, and when she pulled away, I let her go. "How dare I what?" I asked.

"You thought I just left you there for dead? You thought I didn't care? Did you even stop to think how hard that was for me to do? It's good to know you think I'm some type of monster," she screamed at me, wiping her tears and smearing her makeup.

I tried to embrace her, but she was having nothing to do with it. "No! You don't get to do that, you don't deserve to." She turned away, folding her arms across her chest.

Lilly approached, put her arm around Andie Rae, and held her as she wept. The others put their heads down and said nothing. From their reaction, I knew they understood how much pain Andie Rae had in her heart. I took away from that moment that sometimes people do not want advice or to be fixed as much as they simply want someone to listen and hold them. I didn't say a word either, and if I was being honest with myself, I really didn't know what to say.

"What is all the noise about?" Hayden demanded to know before he saw me.

It went dead silent, and I could hear the floorboards squeak with each step he took towards me. He was so mad that I could feel the heat coming off his body. He wore a blank gaze, his fists were clenched, and his hands were trembling.

"Well, well, well … look, everyone, our deliverer has returned. I see you finally got your tail out from between your legs, pansy," he said, standing nose to nose with me.

"It's good to see you too, Hayden."

"What do you want?"

"I wanted to make things right and to say I'm sorry I doubted you, Andie Rae," I said, turning towards her.

"The best thing you can do is just turn around and get out of here," Hayden said, pushing me by the chest.

Bear stood up and got between us. "Settle down, boys, y'all always acting like you pissed in each other's Cheerios," he said, trying to drive Hayden back.

"I'm not in the mood, Bear," Hayden said, pushing past him.

"Well, that was as useful as a sidesaddle on a pig." Bear returned to his stool. He took his hat off to scratch his head.

Hayden grabbed a hold of me, and instead of making a smart remark or getting angry, I closed my eyes and patiently waited for yet another pounding to take place. When he picked me up my shirt lifted and exposed my stomach. He must have been able to see the deep blue bruises I was still healing from. I heard Lilly gasp. Hayden saw the walloping I had taken recently and apparently decided it made little sense to add more to my already battered body. He dropped me and signaled Doc to take a look at me. Doc had me remove my shirt and turn around so he could get a full look at my upper body.

"Seems like someone really did a number on you," Doc said, pulling bandages out of his backpack. Wrapping them tightly around my ribs, he concluded, "You'll be okay in a few more days. This will just help with the pain."

"What happened?" Hayden asked.

"Revenge."

"For what?" Lilly inquired.

"For sticking up for the little guy, for getting involved with you all, for a bunch of things."

"Who did it?" Hayden asked, grabbing a soda and taking a seat at the bar.

"The guys at school who were at the zoo," I said, putting my shirt on. "They cornered me in the gym locker room. There were too many of them to fight and I had no way of running."

"So, you stood there and took that kind of beating?" Toby said.

Taking a seat at the bar, I gave the only answer I thought was right. "Some things are worth standing up for, and sometimes, you have to pay a price for it."

Nodding in agreement, Hayden put down his soda and asked Andie Rae to go check on dinner. I think he sensed she was still very upset. She didn't answer him; she put her head down and walked out of the room with her hands in her pockets.

"I'll go check on her," Lilly said, following her out of the room.

"So now what?" Doc asked, packing up the supplies he'd taken out to tend to me.

I pulled the note from my pocket and let them in on it. "I got this off Jack and his group at school. It has an address with tomorrow's date on it. I figured it would be where they attack next."

Hayden took the piece of paper out of my hand and looked it over for a second. He stood up and paced back and forth, staring at it for another minute. Turning, he said, "Toby, Doc, go check it out."

"Roger, roger," Toby said, picking up his jacket and tossing Doc his car keys.

Doc took the note out of Hayden's hand and read the address. "I know the area, it's in Plant City. Quick shot up Interstate Four, right off Park Road."

Pointing at both of them Hayden said, "Safety, shadows, and surveillance. Nothing else, you two understand?"

They nodded and headed out the door. Hayden grabbed his soda and went to the back of the shop to check in on the girls. I got up to leave when Bear called out to me.

"Where are you going, slick?"

"Hmm, I don't think Andie Rae really wants me around."

"Sometimes I think your brain rattles around like a BB in a boxcar."

Shaking my head and holding up my arms I asked, "What the heck does that mean, Bear?"

He leaned back, putting his elbows on the counter, and said, "It means sometimes I feel you can just be plain dumb." He came around the bar and put both hands on my shoulders. "She's happier than ol' Blue layin' on the porch chewin' on a big ol' catfish head."

Seeing my confusion he clarified. "Trust me, son, she's tickled to see you. Just give her some time, she has a lot built up inside. She'll come around."

"I hope you're right."

He patted me on the back and said, "Now, we have ham sandwiches to eat, crates to unload, and my favorite alien movie to watch."

We walked to the side storage room where he had the crates stacked, an LED projector hooked up to his laptop, and a nice spread of sandwiches on a table. I made my way over to the crates and was shocked to see what was in there. Military grade weapons including M16A4s, Beretta M9s, AK-74s, MP5Ks, FN F2000s and some of the SPAS-12 models.

"How in the world … and why in the world do you all have these?"

He took a bite of his first ham sandwich, put his finger up while he swallowed the behemoth piece, wiped his mouth, and said, "After watching a flick, it hit me: all of them soldiers ran in there and fought those aliens with some major gear." He took another bite, inhaled it, and continued. "So I thought—we're fighting for real, so why do it with shotguns and handguns and such, when we should have the real deal. I pitched it to Hayden, and that old salty dog had me order a bunch."

I walked over to the table, chose a much smaller sandwich than Bear had, then took a seat next to him as he started the movie.

"When we're done with our first helping, we need to start loading clips if we're going to go hunting tomorrow."

He handed me a box full of silver bullets and a bunch of different clips to start loading when I was done. We ate and watched the movie for a while with Bear role playing during every fighting sequence. The thing that still struck me was the carefree attitude they all had towards death. I was still terrified at that , and seeing how they'd upgraded their arsenal told me they were trying to eliminate the threat once and for all. As I started to punch bullets into the clips, my thoughts turned to Doc and Toby, hoping the note would lead to something that would benefit us in—it was now apparent to me— this war.

Chapter 11
The Big White House

I woke up to find Lilly standing over me with breakfast. Sitting up, I looked around and found Bear sleeping next to me with fully loaded clips of ammunition all around him. He let out a few monstrous snores—his large frame gasped for air as he slept. I rubbed my eyes and turned towards Lilly who took a seat next to me on the floor and handed me a plate of pancakes and a glass of milk.

"What time is it?" I asked before diving into the delicious cakes on my plate.

"It's about nine in the morning. We're waiting for Toby and Doc to get back from the assignment out in Plant City," she said before sipping on her coffee.

"How is Andie Rae?"

"She's good. She was really upset that you thought that little of her. I tried to tell you at the hospital that you got her all wrong, but you wouldn't listen."

I put my plate down and scratched my head violently with both hands. "Yeah, it's a problem I've had all my life—jump to conclusions and judge before I hear people out."

"She'll be okay. Just give her some time." She stood up. "Do me a favor and wake Bear—Hayden will want to have a meeting when they get back," she said and walked out of the storage room.

I rapidly scooped up my plate and finished my breakfast before waking Bear up. Looking around the room, I was very impressed with how much prep work we were able to accomplish last night. There were stacks upon stacks of full magazines waiting to be paired up with their assigned gun. I gave Bear a soft boot in his butt to try and stir him. After a few more kicks, he jumped up and looked around like he was still in a light daze.

"I'll be on you like a hobo on a hoagie," he shouted with his fists in the air.

"Bear, calm down, it's just me," I said, putting my hands over his and lowering them. "We need to get up and get ready to meet with Hayden."

He stretched and let out a bellowing yawn before standing up. "You need to be more careful waking a fella up." Adjusting himself and having a fit of the shakes, he said, "I got to whiz like a racehorse."

Bear made his way to the bathroom and I joined the others out in the main bar area. Doc and Toby had returned, and everyone was finishing up breakfast. After completing his business in the bathroom, Bear came into the room, seized what was left of the massive stack of pancakes, and poured a heap of syrup over them. He carved out giant mouthfuls and shoved them into his mouth.

With his trap still full of the pancakes, he turned to Andie Rae and said, "Perfect as always, honey. You know you can cook almost as well as my mama."

Andie Rae smiled and thanked him. Comparing her to his mama was the highest compliment I believed Bear could give anyone. Lilly and Toby started to clean up the bar area for Hayden who was bringing in a large map he normally clipped up behind the bar. I decided to be useful and wiped the bar down with a wet rag, mostly to clean up the mess Bear had made with the abundance of maple syrup he used. When I was done, I tossed Bear the rag to wipe his hands off so he could help Hayden finish hanging up the map. After returning to our seats, Hayden gestured for Toby and Doc to give us a rundown on what they found.

"The address led us to a big white house with a large front yard," Doc said, drawing out the area on a piece of paper he had with him. "Each side is well covered, with a trailer park on the left and brush on the right."

"Was there any evidence this is our target?" Andie Rae asked.

"Absolutely. There were dark vans pulling up all night, and individuals shackled and gagged being dragged into the house against their will," Toby answered. He blew on his glasses so he could clean them.

"Sounds like they were fixin' their spread," Bear said in disgust.

"It does, and I think the best approach will be from the brush," Doc said, walking over to the map.

"What do you think the best rally point would be?" Hayden asked.

Doc, pointing out the tall strawberry water tower in the park, responded, "This would be the best place to meet and park our vehicles." He took a pencil and started to draw our route to the house on the map. "From there, under the cover of darkness, we can make our way through the park to the brush line. Once we make sure we're clear, we can gain entrance through the side door."

"Any guards outside when the vans were not there?" Lilly asked.

"Not one person stayed outside when the vans were not there," Toby responded.

Hayden started to pace back and forth, not saying a word. We were all looking for him to make the call and, after a few minutes, he slammed his fist onto the counter and looked at us, smiling. "Time to go hunting, boys and girls. You know what to do, let's go get ready."

Everyone headed into separate rooms, following the routines they were used to for these types of events. I hurried off the restroom after securing a change of clothes and toothbrush from Lilly. The butterflies made their presence known in my stomach as I washed up. I knew I was doing the right thing, but, unlike the others, I was still scared and worried that I just might meet my maker later that evening. After showering, I got out, wrapped a towel around me, and brushed my teeth. When I spun around to grab my clothes, Andie

Rae opened the door and walked in, still talking to someone in the hall, right into me.

"Oh ... I'm so sorry, I didn't realize you were still in here," she said with her hands on my chest.

"No worries. I was just getting my clothes and I'll be out of here."

Andie Rae slowly backed towards the door and I could tell she was eyeing me up and down. "That's okay Connell, I'll go use the other one," she said.

"Are you sure? I'm just about finished, I promise."

She giggled while opening the door and said, "I'm sure, sorry again."

Chuckling, I put my clothes on, thinking we'd made some progress—she didn't slap me this time. I made my way back to the storage room where everyone was busy working. I helped them decide which weapons we would use, loaded extra clips in our trench coats, and watched Toby pull out his orbs and carefully place them on his vest. Those things scared the crap out of me, mainly because I always feared that he would mishandle one, leading to some severe damage.

With the prep work done, everyone went off to do their own thing for the rest of the day. Andie Rae and Lilly were cooking and listening to tunes on the radio, Doc and Toby were playing chess, and Hayden and Bear were outside, Bear enjoying some of his chew and Hayden shooting some basketball. I decided I would call the one person who never doubted me, who I loved dearly, and who was always there for me: my grandmother. It was one of her bad days; she thought I was my dad. I tried to correct her a few times at first; however, the joy in her voice and listening to what she was saying always gave me a new insight into my dad and how he grew up. We talked for hours, and, towards the end of the conversation, I told her I loved her and would see her soon. She encouraged me to hurry home, be safe, and reminded me that she loved me with all her heart. Hanging up the phone I let out a big sigh and wiped the tears out of my eyes.

"You okay?" Lilly asked as she approached.

"Yeah, I was just talking to my grandmother," I said, walking towards the backdoor to check on what Bear and Hayden were up to. "She's not doing too well and she's all I have left, so it's hard."

Lilly took a hold of my hand and walked with me. She didn't say anything, but I enjoyed the company. It was clear that she completely understood where I was coming from. It was her and her sister, and they had no other family. I was so wrapped up in my own needs and wants, that I forgot every time we went out they could lose each other for good, and that had to weigh heavily on their minds. I smiled at her and moved my hand to wrap around her. She gripped my hand with her right as it lay hanging over her shoulder. She smiled in return, and I squeezed her tightly to let her know how much I appreciated her.

Opening the back door, we could hear Bear and Hayden talking. "I'm telling you, Hayden, sometimes I think she could fall into an outhouse and she'd still come up smelling like a rose."

"Sorry to interrupt your compelling conversation, boys, but dinner is ready," Lilly announced.

"Hot dog, I'm so hungry I could eat a cat turd fried in snot," Bear exclaimed as he stood up, yanked up his pants and charged past us into the shop.

"Thanks Lilly, I'll be right there," Hayden said, picking up the spit bottle Bear left behind.

We made our way to the table where there was a marvelous spread of fried chicken, collard greens, shrimp and grits, pimento cheese, and a host of other items. Sweet tea was bountiful as were cobblers of all sorts. The aroma was one that could put a smile on the most uptight person. Taking our seats, Bear went to start filling his plate, and Andie Rae slapped him. It was clear that we were to wait on everyone to get to the table first. Hayden came in with Bear's bottle and tossed it into the trash can before taking a seat at the head of the table. Everyone took hands—well, everyone except Hayden—and Toby led us in grace. It was a beautiful prayer that asked not only for our protection, but also strength to endure the burdens of nights like tonight.

"Thank you for such an outstanding meal, ladies," Toby said, seizing a large helping of fried chicken.

"Well thanks, Toby, I appreciate that," Lilly said, watching Bear wipe his mouth with his sleeve and feasting on the mountain of food on his plate.

"You know he appreciates it, Lilly," Hayden said in Bear's defense.

"What about you?" Andie Rae asked, smirking.

Hayden took another bite, winked at both girls, and answered, "Complete crap, I wouldn't feed it to my dog."

The girls smiled and went back to eating. I found it strange that, even with this group, Hayden had to maintain such a tough guy mentality. The only reason I could think of was that he was the glue that held everything together. If he showed emotion, if he showed vulnerability, if he showed any fear, it would affect everyone. We ate, and the mood was somber at best, mainly because no one knew if they would see the sun again or if they would be lucky enough to escape from death's door one more time. I never asked how many others there had been over the years and dared not ask that question tonight.

With the meal all wrapped up, the team gathered and started to put on their gear. It was just like always, Hayden sitting on the end of the bar keeping to himself while we all helped each other load up. Once we were done, we conducted the traditional prayer and waited for further instructions from Hayden. He got off his stool and walked over to the group. Maybe I hadn't noticed it before because I was always in a panic, but he put his hand on each person's shoulder and nodded at them. When he got to me he stared for a moment, then finally did the same for me. It felt like a huge weight had been lifted off my chest. It appeared we had made it to the next phase of our relationship. Perhaps that meant he would actually start using my name; it didn't take long for him to answer that question.

We made our way outside to the cars, and Hayden started to give us instructions. "Doc and Toby, y'all have the Wildcat. Girls, you're with me in the Barracuda." Looking over at me he continued, "Pansy, you're with Bear."

I turned to Bear and asked, "Are you ready?"

He laughed, placed some chaw in his lip, and started to climb up into his truck. "Does a one-legged duck swim in circles?"

I shook my head, snickered, and joined him in the passenger seat. When he turned over the engine, it let out a loud roar like a lion protecting its territory. Pulling out, he turned on his radio, and we rocked all the way up Interstate Four listening to a multitude of songs including "Are You Going My Way" by Lenny Kravitz.

After about a thirty-minute drive, we pulled off at Park Road, turned through the sports complex, and parked under the giant strawberry tower. The sun was almost set, so we quickly did our last-minute checks and headed across the park towards the bushes. The area was deserted and had an eerie feel to it. There were no animals around, no birds in the air, and no wind blowing. All we could hear were our own footsteps. While no one said a word, I knew most of us were thinking the same thing; something did not feel right.

Everyone was looking around, and I could see beads of sweat forming on Doc's forehead. When we were under the cover of the shrubberies, we knelt down and surveyed the area.

"I don't like this, Hayden, it's too quiet," Doc said, wiping off his brow.

Hayden looked around and smelled the air. "I can smell them, Doc, they are here."

"But there's no movement at all. This place was a lot busier a couple days ago," Toby answered.

Hayden turned to us and must have seen panic on a few faces. "We have been here dozens of times, guys. Stay close and we'll all be okay." He put his hand on Doc's shoulder. "Trust me."

Doc put his head down and let out a deep sigh. "Okay, Hayden, you make the call."

Hayden turned to Lilly. "I want you to stay here and be our eyes and ears, okay?"

"No, I want to be with you guys and my sister," she said in protest.

"Listen to me, Lilly, we need to know if anyone comes in behind us. It is critical we have you out here covering our backs," Hayden said, looking at Andie Rae, signaling her to help convince Lilly.

Picking up on the cue, Andie Rae added, "He's right, Lilly, and besides—there's no one I trust more to have my back." She smiled and hugged Lilly. "I'll be okay, I promise."

Lilly teared up as she hugged her sister back and nodded in agreement, rubbing away her tears. "Be safe," she said to the team before crawling under one of the bushes with her gun, cell phone, and binoculars.

The rest of us made our way out of the tree line and towards the side door of the house. It was locked and had a large deadbolt on it. Hayden looked over at Toby and Doc who could only shrug in response. After thinking for a second, Hayden signaled Bear to go and check the front door while we waited. I glanced up, watching the sky make its final transition to night with the bright full moon providing light for us to operate. Bear peaked around the corner and signaled for us to move. We swiftly made our way to the front door and knelt down, waiting for further directions.

Bear, sweating profusely, started to give us instructions. "When we go in, there ain't nobody in sight. It looks like no one has been here in a hot minute, and the boards make a lot of noise when y'all be walking on them."

Hayden turned to us and signaled to follow him in. With the large red double doors squealing as they opened, we spread out in the huge dark and dusty room looking for any sign of movement. We took a minute and turned on our rifle-mounted flashlights to give us some visibility. As we slowly made our through each room, it was apparent that the owners had long disappeared, and no one had kept up the majestic white house. In each room, it was the same scene: lots of covered furniture, dirt piled up on the floor, and dust so thick it would make the shop feel like a five-star hotel. Continuing to sniff at his surroundings, Hayden led us to the library and started to look around the bookcases.

"The scent is strongest in here," he said, looking around, perplexed.

Doc, pushing and pulling on individual bookcases, said, "Come on, help me, there has to be some type of entrance somewhere in here."

Everyone looked around and pulled or pushed on everything in sight. Toby, who was staring at an extra-large area rug that looked out of place, pulled it back to check out what was underneath. Struggling with the heavy rug, he whispered, "Bear, I could use some help, please."

Bear made his way over and with one arm holding his shotgun. He pulled the rug back with little to no effort. Strangely, there was not too much dust kicked up from this, which suggested it had recently been moved. Staring at the wood planks on the floor, Toby noticed a notch in one. He bent over and put his hand on it as we gathered around him with our guns pointing down at the floor. He pulled on the notch, and a large area of the floor opened up to reveal a ladder leading down into an uninviting pit. From the limited view we had with our flashlights, it looked very tight and slippery, with running water on the rocky walls and floors.

Hayden bent over and smelled for a scent. He came up quickly, wiping his nose, and said, "This is it, guys, they're down there."

The team paused and looked at each other. Doc spoke up. "Hayden, we don't fight in close quarters, remember. You always said that gives them the advantage."

Looking frustrated, Hayden ignored Doc and started to bark out his orders. "I will take the lead, and Bear, Andie, and pansy get the middle." He paused for a moment and looked at Doc. "I'm counting on you, Doc. You and Toby, have our backs."

Toby stared at Doc, waiting for an answer, and when one was not forthcoming, he looked down the pit one last time, spat, and said, "Okay. Doc and I have this."

Doc clearly wasn't pleased and didn't agree with Hayden; however, he was not going to allow Toby to go down there without him. We made our way down the long wooden ladder and regrouped at the bottom. It was cold, wet, and very dark. The only light we had was our flashlights, and they only allowed us to see in the direction we pointed them. We could hear movement in the distance and started to make our way slowly towards it. We had to walk single file as there was barely enough room to turn our guns and keep aim. With each step, I was agreeing with Doc more and more—this was indeed a bad idea. It was like a maze of never-ending tunnels, and Hayden would change direction on occasion based on what he smelled. I could hear Andie Rae whispering to Lilly via Bluetooth from time to time that we were okay, just to keep her at ease. Walking for another hundred yards or so, Toby's flashlight started to give him trouble, so he and Doc stopped for a second.

I turned to them and asked, "You all okay?"

Doc bent down, took off his bag and started to rummage through it. "Yeah, just looking for my spare light."

Toby, who was taking off his broken flashlight, paused as if he heard something. Picking up his gun and looking around, he would have had trouble seeing because of the faulty light. "Do you all hear that?" he shouted.

Hayden stopped the group and started to make his way back to Doc and Toby in a hurry, but it was too late. Something leaped out of a side tunnel and knocked Doc over, tearing into his flesh. Toby screamed and unleashed as many rounds at it as he could with his light flickering off and on. The rest of us started to run back towards them as the howls began to swell around us. Hayden leaped passed Toby and into the creature that was ripping Doc apart. While he fought the beast, a second one came from an opposite tunnel and knocked Toby over. It dug its huge fangs into Toby's stomach, and he let out an ear-piercing scream. Bear emptied his shotgun shells into the beast and drove it off Toby.

"You gonna be okay, little buddy, hang with us," Bear said, desperately trying to cover Toby's wounds with his hands.

With the howls picking up, Bear looked around with his flashlight and saw our worst nightmare. Scores of them were heading our way from the direction we'd entered, which meant we had no way out.

"Boys and girls, we need to move as fast as a sailor on a four-hour pass, if you get my meaning," he said, picking up Toby.

Andie Rae picked up Doc's bag and followed Bear. I took a hold of Doc by the arm and started to pull him, but I quickly fell back on my butt. Getting to my feet, I shined my light on Doc and found he'd been torn in half.

With no time to mourn my friend, I flashed my light down the tunnel one more time and screamed at Hayden, "We need to move now, come on."

Hayden bit off the head of the werewolf he was fighting and looked down the tunnel at the mob of monsters madly making their way towards us. He started to sprint back towards me, and we both took off, trying to catch up to the others.

Zigzagging through different tunnels, we found an enclosed room with two oversized oak doors. Laying Toby down on the ground, Bear rushed over to help Hayden, now back in his human form, and me close and latch the doors.

"What the heck was that," I shouted as I turned and leaned on the doors.

"Calm down, pansy, we need to keep our heads about us," Hayden said.

I leaped away from the door and grabbed a hold of him. "What about Doc, why didn't you listen?"

He did not fight back and simply said, "I made a mistake. I broke my own rules and it cost Doc his life." Pointing over at Toby he said, "Are we going to try to save Toby, or would you rather continue to waste time fighting?"

I let him go and rushed over to assist Andie Rae with Toby. The beast's razor-sharp fangs had left Toby's torso in the condition of a gutted fish that was ready to be consumed. He squealed as the beast's saliva dissolved his tissue, exposing the bone. Andie Rae put pressure on his wounds with some bandages from Doc's bag while I shot him up with morphine. We sat with him, holding his hand and trying to console him.

"What happened to Doc?" he asked.

Andie Rae looked up at me and I shook my head. She said, "He got out and is with Lilly."

"Good, I was scared that he didn't make it," Toby said, gasping for air.

Andie Rae wept as she tried to comfort Toby, and I put my arm around her. She did not resist but turned her head and leaned it into my chest, sobbing. Hayden and Bear monitored the door. Looking over, I could hear the monstrous howls as the werewolves thrashed their claws against the enormous oak structure. After numerous assaults, it became evident the old wooden doors would give in to their demands shortly. Everybody knew when that occurred it would equate to our demise. The thought of being slaughtered by the very creatures we'd sworn to eradicate sickened everyone. Patiently waiting for death to come and claim us, I held Andie Rae a little tighter. Hayden paced in front of the massive door, never taking his eyes off it. The rage in his soul was so mighty that it was evident to everyone, but it had also clouded his judgment. Otherwise we would not be here right now.

Bear started to load his shotgun again with shaking hands and proclaimed to us, "Will you look at that? I'm as nervous as a long-tailed cat in a room full of rocking chairs."

Hayden walked over and put his hand on his shoulder, took his shotgun, and finished loading it for him. Bear took the opportunity to sit on the ground with his back against the wall and wiped the sweat out of his eyes.

Distressed at the sight of Toby, I bowed my head and silently prayed. Andie Rae gently took a hold of my hand, leaned in, and kissed me for the first time. What luck for a guy to have; now that I was about to die, the girl of my dreams decides to show her feelings towards me. I went to speak, but she put her finger over my lips and slowly shook her head, no. Understanding that this wasn't the time or place for such a conversation, I returned my attention to the door. With each strike, she moved closer to me, and I could feel her heart racing with anticipation of the mayhem that was looming.

After endless battering, the heavy oak door cracked, and we were now within the sight of our enemies. Andie Rae let go of my hand and got to her feet. She raised her weapon, determined to go out on her terms. While a tear fell from her face, I heard her say softly, "I love you, Lilly."

Toby grabbed me by my shirt and pulled me down towards him. "Help me get to my feet," he groaned.

I assisted him to his feet, and he grabbed for one of his orbs. "Hayden," he screamed, waving the orb towards him.

Hayden rushed over and took Toby out of my arms. "Are you sure, Toby?"

He let out a painful laugh and said, "My cards have been dealt. Promise me you'll get them out of here."

Fighting back tears, Hayden responded in a cracked voice, "I promise, Toby." Turning him towards the door he whispered in Toby's ear, "I'm sorry."

Smiling and turning towards him, Toby said, "It's all good. I'm ready to go."

Hayden nodded and shouted for us all to get behind him. Bear covered Andie Rae with his large frame, and I stood in front of them with my gun at the ready. Toby mustered what strength he had left and pulled the pin on the orb he was holding. Hayden ran towards the beasts and pushed Toby into the splintered door. There was a loud blast; it blinded me, and the force of the explosion flung me backwards. I lost sight of my team as I hit the ground. Barely conscious and blinded by dense black smoke, I listened to the sound of death claiming numerous creatures around me. With no strength to protest, I felt something drag me off to an unknown destination. I felt myself slowly fade into unconsciousness, trying to recall how I came to be in this hellish place.

Chapter 12
Is that you?

When I regained consciousness, the room was spinning rapidly, and I had to grab my throbbing head to ease the pain. My eyesight was blurry, my shirt was missing, and I seemed to have bandages around my elbow and chest. Moving about in what I now recognized as a cot, I still felt that cold, eerie sensation we experienced in the tunnels. With every movement, my head pounded so heavily that I felt like vomiting. I could hear someone in the next room fumbling around and talking themselves into a frenzy. Sitting up, I felt sharp pains going through my chest, which had to be the result of the orbs.

"Toby," I whispered to myself, remembering what happened.

I looked around and found my shirt on a chair in the corner. Clutching my chest, I hurried over to it, shaking the cobwebs out of my head, and hurriedly put it back on. It had some holes in it where the shrapnel from the explosion that had caused my wounds most likely hit me. Standing up caused me to feel a tad light-headed, and I had to brace myself against the wall. I inched my way towards the doorway, wondering what happened to Andie Rae and the others. I peered out of the doorway and could not believe what I saw.

I stumbled out of the door. "Kevin?"

Looking up from something he was working on, there was my best friend since kindergarten. He was unclean, needed a shave, and smelled awful.

"Ahh ... Connell, how are you feeling?" he asked, clasping his hands together with a smile that revealed brown teeth.

Looking him up and down, I said, "What the heck happened to you?"

Laughing and nervously running his hands through his matted hair, he bent over a flame and signaled for me to come closer. Looking around furtively, he whispered, "Freedom."

He started to giggle and returned to working on some type of science project that seemed to involve blood. I shook my head in disbelief at first, and then anger set in. I made my way over to the other side of the table where he was working and slammed my fist down.

"I thought you were dead," I shouted crossly at him, forgetting about how much pain I was in.

Jumping back in a panic, he rushed over to the door, opened it, looked around, and closed it again. "Be quiet, or they'll hear you," he said nervously.

Joining him at the door and continuing to ignore my pain, I grabbed him by the arms, shook him, and asked, "Who are you talking about? What is the matter with you?"

He screamed, and pulled away from me, ran back over to his desk, and carried on working, murmuring anxiously to himself. Feeling dizzy, I had to lean against the wall so as not to fall over. I grabbed a nearby stool and joined Kevin at the table in order to rest and find out what had happened to him.

"Hey, Kevin, you have to help me here. The last time I saw you, you were begging me not to let go, then you just disappeared inside with a bunch of monsters."

"Monsters?" Kevin retorted. "Not monsters, but misunderstood gods with the ability for immortality." Rubbing his hands together, he looked up at me and continued. "We have been so wrong about them. They are not the enemy, but those who hunt them are."

Shaking my head in disbelief and picking up one of his vials of blood, I said, "So Lilly and I are your enemies?"

He snatched the vial out of my hand and shrieked at me, "Don't touch that." He carefully placed the vial back in its case with the others. "Yes, you are now, both of you."

"Why did you save me if I'm your enemy?" I asked, sickened by his comment.

He paused, looked at me, and I saw my friend for the first time. "I owed you for all you had done for me. But now we're even."

Rubbing my hands through my hair in frustration I asked, "Why are you acting so different than Jack and the rest?"

Kevin cackled. "Those simple-minded fools miss the bigger picture, the potential of this power. They are simply mites in a world meant for deities."

I looked around the room for any clues. "So what happens now?"

Kevin paused, put his hands on the table, and looked down in silence. I stood up and took a few steps back, waiting to see what he would do. I was not sure if I could ever bring myself to fight him, but it was clear he was not right in the head.

"I let you walk out of here," he said, going back to working on his experiment.

"That's it?" I asked, putting my hands on my hips.

"For now. Then we are even."

He walked over to the door, lifted the latch, opened it, and looked in both directions. "You're safe, just go to the left, stay in the shadows, and it will lead you back to the surface."

I made my way over to the door where he was standing and hesitated. "So this is how you want to end a lifetime of friendship?" I asked, without looking at him.

Expressionless, he responded, "It has to be this way now."

I glanced at him. My birthmark glowed as my temper increased. "Fine, but if you come near the shop, give us away, or hurt Lilly or Andie Rae, I will hunt you down to the ends of the earth and kill you."

Laughing and exposing his brown teeth he replied, "Give the shop away? To who? Those idiots? No, I'm working on something bigger than those simpletons would ever understand."

I put my good arm on his shoulder and said, "Goodbye, Kevin."

He remained silent as I headed down the dark tunnel in the direction he told me to go. I looked back a few times to see if he would change his mind and follow me, but he disappeared back into the room he was working in. Hugging the wall and staying low to keep in the shadows, I felt tears building up in my eyes. I could not decide what was worse—thinking Kevin was dead or knowing he was now my enemy. I remembered what he said on the bus that first day and would never have imagined how right he was about our lives being very different this year.

I could hear rumbling and a lot of yelling in the distance. The voices sounded familiar, which made me extremely nervous. Wiping the tears out of my eyes, I tried to get Kevin out of my head; I could not afford to be careless right now. Arrogance and sloppiness had already cost my friends their lives tonight and, while I would miss them, I was in no rush to meet up with them again. Making my way along the wet, dark path, I saw some light ahead and inched my way closer to the corner. As I approached the overhang where the voices were coming from, I decided to crawl the rest of the way and get as close to them as possible to overhear what I could. I saw the hooded figure from the first night in Ybor City, the fat bus driver, and Jack's group. It looked like they were burying some of the werewolves that didn't make it under the cavern we were in. Funny thing was, unlike the movies, they hadn't changed back to their human form. Instead, they retained the bodily form they were in on death. The mass grave was huge, and they were dumping dead carcasses in there; it seemed they were stacked three or four high.

"Wow, Toby, you really did a number on them," I murmured, looking around.

I could see Jack sitting in the corner, crying. It seemed he'd lost a lot of his pack tonight, and Tammy was nowhere in sight, which was odd. She was connected by the hip to Jack at all times. Perhaps that was why he was so upset—maybe she didn't make it. Regardless, I still needed to get myself out of there and find the others. I had no time to worry about Tammy. As I started to crawl away, the hooded figure approached Jack and slapped him across the face. I stopped to enjoy the moment. I couldn't tell what was being said, but the hooded figure was madder than a rabid dog. He dragged Jack by the hair over to the bodies and stuck his face into the pit, yelling. I guessed their plan had not gone as well as they hoped. Perhaps the others got out. While I would have enjoyed nothing more than to watch Jack get some of what he dished to the outcasts, I needed to keep moving.

Standing back up was a chore—sharp pains ran through my chest and arm. I made it to my feet with the aid of the cold rocky wall, and hugged the shadows as I made my way through the maze of tunnels. I started to wonder if Kevin was setting me up, but he was never one to lie. Even as he made it clear that we were enemies, he assured me he owed me this last favor. Nervously, and without much light, I eventually found my way to a set of stairs. Did I go up them or was I supposed to go past them and follow the tunnel?

"What the heck do I do now?" I asked myself, trying to see where the steps led.

I started to climb the stairs, but something grabbed at my ankle through the steps.

Leaping off the staircase, I screamed in a panic and put my fists up. As beads of sweat formed on my forehead, a figure emerged from the underneath the stairs and into the dim light. It was Tammy, signaling me to be quiet.

"Calm down, Connell, it's only me," she said as she approached.

"Only you?" I sneered. "Aren't you with the heap of dung that attacked us?"

She sighed and pulled her long blonde hair back into a bun. "Yes, but not by choice."

"What do you mean?" I asked, lowering my fists slightly.

"Jack … well, Jack tricked me and told me I had to do it to help him, that we would be together forever, and I believed him. I never wanted to hurt anyone, and I hate what I am."

Seeing the tears stream down her face, I could not help but feel compassion for her. Jack was just the right amount of jerk that I could see this happening. "I'm sorry, Tammy, I had no idea." I did the only thing I knew that helped during this type of situation: I hugged her. She squeezed me back and sobbed uncontrollably.

"I lost a lot of friends tonight, and I know you did too," she whimpered. "I just want it to stop."

Thinking about Toby, Doc, Kevin, and Melanie, I said, "Yeah, me too."

"Can y'all please stop the love fest?" a voice moaned from the darkness.

Tammy let me go and pulled me toward the stairs. "Oh, snap, I forgot."

"Forgot you were just helping me two minutes ago," the irritated voice said.

Hunkering down below the steps, in really bad shape, was Hayden.

"You look like a hot mess," I said, looking at all the cuts and dried blood on him.

"Thanks, pansy, you always know the exact thing to say," he responded sarcastically, holding his ribs. "Seems like Toby was a little too good with those orbs of his—they nearly blew me apart."

"The others?" I asked.

"She's fine, pansy, Bear got her out," he said.

"How do you know that?"

"Because we were all together at first, but I was slowing them down, so I sent them ahead, and I went looking for your dumb face. What happened to you anyway?"

I thought about it for a second. I wanted to protect Lilly from the pain and Kevin from Hayden. "Long story, not sure I could explain it all right now." Looking back up at Tammy, I asked, "How do you fit into all of this?"

"She's the informant, you idiot," Hayden snapped. "She was the one providing us and you all the clues."

Thinking about that, it was so clear; how could I have missed it? "She was the one you and Bear were talking about in the back alley."

"You know, sometimes I wonder what Andie sees in you," he said as Tammy helped him to his feet. "Right now, you and I need to get out of here."

I put his arm around my shoulder, looked at Tammy and asked, "What about you?"

She smiled at me. "You don't have to worry about me. I'll have Jack eating out of my hands in minutes."

Hayden nodded at her, and Tammy and I exchanged smiles before I helped Hayden up the wooden stairs. We were both struggling to climb the handful of steps—each move hurt either one of us or both of us at the same time. Approaching the top, we could see small rays of light coming through the wooden doors. We pushed them open and found ourselves at the back of the house, leaving what appeared to be a storm shelter. Hugging the walls of the house and looking out for guards, we made our way back to the tree line. Hayden struggled to get back over the fence, so I shoved him and he landed hard.

"Dang it, what is wrong with you, pansy?" he growled as he rolled on the floor in pain.

Hopping the fence and wincing in pain myself, I grimaced. "Stop being a big baby."

Hayden sat up and leaned against the fence. "Not bad."

"Not bad, what?" I asked.

He chuckled. "Dang, man, I can't even give you a small compliment without you questioning it. You did okay in there, alright? You took care of yourself and kept your head about you and got us out."

Puzzled, I simply said, "Thank you, I think?"

"Come on, pansy, we need to keep moving," he said, struggling to his feet.

We wrestled our way back through the tree line and into the park. It was a weird situation at best. A lot of people were out for their morning jogs, and here we are all battered up and bloody coming out of the trees. I could see the joggers' cell phones out, and many of them were making phone calls. I imagined they were calling the police, which was the last thing we needed. We moved as quickly as we could back towards the Wildcat, which Doc and Toby had driven. I quickly opened the door, and Hayden dropped down into the passenger seat. I went to close the door, and he grabbed me by the shirt.

"Under the trunk is a magnet with a spare key," he said.

I quickly retrieved the key—I could hear sirens in the background. I jumped into the driver's seat, ignoring my pain, and hurriedly started the car. I pulled the Wildcat out so fast it kicked up a cloud of dirt. I slammed it into drive and took off like a raging lunatic, regardless of the limited vision I had through the dust. Speeding through the park, I made my way back onto the interstate heading towards Ybor.

"Don't go to the shop. We need to disappear for a while," Hayden commanded.

"Disappear?" I asked.

"Yes, those fools have a description of the car and we can't allow it to lead them back to the shop."

Nodding my head in agreement I asked, "Okay, where to?"

"Head north and let's get to Bear's place," he directed.

Turning onto Interstate Seventy-Five, I could hear the sirens fade, but I knew he was right. It was too dangerous to be at the shop, Chamberlain, or even at Grandma's with the Wildcat. Besides, we both needed some time to heal and figure out what our next steps would be. There was no denying that this would have shaken the team to its core, even before I'd seen Bear and Andie Rae. I could only hope they were safe.

Chapter 13
Acceptance

Morning already – nertz. It had been weeks since Hayden and I made our dash to Bear's house, with no communication whatsoever with anyone. He kept telling me the gang was okay, but right now we needed to lay low, get better, and work on a plan. That consisted of him having me do some absurd exercises, him sitting around drinking something called banana beer, and us getting into arguments with each other. Rolling out of bed, I looked over my body in the mirror and was very happy with how I was healing up. The scars from the orbs were minimal, and, for the first time in days, my body did not feel like it had been hit by a truck.

After showering and getting dressed, I headed to the kitchen for some breakfast. Unlike every other day when I ate by myself, Hayden was actually in the kitchen cooking us something to eat.

Looking up from the skillet Hayden saw me and said, "Good morning, pansy. Breakfast is just about done."

"What's all this? Usually you're still passed out for another hour or two."

Hayden turned off the stove and slid the last omelet onto a plate. He handed me one and took a seat at the bar. "Can't I do something nice and not be questioned about it?"

"No," I responded curtly.

He laughed, shook his head in agreement, and started to eat his masterpiece. I had to admit it was one of the best omelets I'd ever tasted. Wiping my mouth, I reached over and grabbed the book I'd been thumbing through from Bear's den. It was a Celtic book on Filtiarn. I figured since that was the character the gang gave me in my role-playing group, it wouldn't hurt me to understand more about it.

Taking a swig of milk, Hayden noticed the book and asked, "What do you have there?"

"This? It's a book about some wolf lord named Filtiarn. The group I hang out with at school and play this game with gave me that name." I quickly shut the book and tossed it over to the table. "It's nothing really. I think it's dumb."

Hayden let out an outrageous laugh and slapped me on the back. "I would watch what you say—Filtiarn, she was one wicked lady. She was one of the most powerful, beautiful, and cunning warriors ever in our ranks."

Shaking my head in disbelief, I turned towards him and asked, "Are you telling me this is real, and you knew this person?"

"Well, when you're roughly six thousand years old, there's not much you haven't experienced in your life," he said, finishing up his food.

"Filtiarn was a woman?" I asked.

"No, Filtiarn is a title and the last person to hold it was a woman," he answered, tossing his toast back on his plate.

He got up, took his stuff to the sink, and started to clean up. I could tell he didn't want to talk about it, but, as always, I was not going to let it alone. "So what can you tell me about her?"

"I can tell you she would not appreciate all the tomfoolery that you and your friends include her title with," he answered swiftly, drying off his dish.

"Tomfoolery?"

He turned to face me, wiping his hands on a towel and leaning against the sink. "Yeah, you know like silliness, giddiness, and antics. That sort of thing."

I smirked and took a bite of my toast. "It's clear you do not understand how seriously these guys take this game." I rubbed my hands together over my plate to remove the crumbs from my toast and elaborated. "Trust me, it's their life, and they're very respectful. Even to the point where I think it is pure madness."

"Good to know," he replied.

"So tell me about her."

Hayden threw the towel on the counter, went over to the fridge, and grabbed two banana beers.

"Here, have one," he said, handing me the frosty beverage.

"Wait, you're actually allowing me to have one of your special drinks?"

"You are a wolf man, right?"

I had to agree. I took the lid off and watched as the warm air turned the glass bottle frosty. I took a swig of the yellowish creamy liquid, and, to my surprise, it was marvelous. It had a banana flavor mixed with coconut and a hint of lime to it.

"That's really good," I said before taking another swig.

"Yeah, it's a brew that was especially made by the townspeople for us. It was their way of showing appreciation for our protection." He took another drink. "It's the one thing that still brings me comfort and joy in this world."

"Why is that?" I asked.

"Okay, pansy, I guess you've put up with my abuse long enough to deserve an answer," he said, grinning. He jumped up onto the kitchen countertop.

Hayden spent the next hour telling me all about himself and the clan of wolf men he was a member of. They were taught that people were good creatures that lacked the internal light to guide their decisions. The Elders thought it was a virtue to use fear as a way to keep people in line: fear of their wolf men. Back then, wars, corruption, and crime were not commonplace because justice was served by our kind providing an example for others to see. In exchange for their good deeds, the wolf men protected their people from attacks by interlopers.

He explained that Filtiarn was a title given to the best of our ranks and passed down from generation to generation. The Filtiarn who oversaw them during his time was Nadia. She was small in stature, but she had the heart of a lion. He recalled her short, dark hair, her bronzed skin, and the numerous freckles on her face. She was always dressed in white and had two white lines tattooed beneath her left eye. They fought alongside each other for centuries, and she was like the field general directing the clan's movements. She had them trained like a well-oiled machine, and the fight was usually over before the other side knew what hit them.

He paused for a moment, wiped a tear from his eye, and took another swig of his banana beer. "Then Kane happened," he said. "She warned me, but I still believed that he just lacked the light to show him the way." He laughed and shook his head. "And that mistake cost her life."

Looking away from him, I struggled to say anything. In a panic, I took another sip and said, "Wow, that sucks."

"Now that is an understatement if I ever heard one," he countered, reaching in the fridge for another bottle.

I wiped by brow and said, "Sorry, Hayden. It seems like she meant a lot to you."

Still looking in the fridge, he simply said, "Yeah, she did."

Understanding this was an off-limits topic, I decided to change direction and ask him something else I had been curious about.

"So, I've heard you all talk about Kane, but what's the deal with this Enoch person?" I asked.

"It's about time you got around to that," he responded, shutting the fridge door.

"What do you mean?"

"I mean that question lets me know that you're all in, that you're part of the team."

Hayden let out a sigh, and began to give me the details. He told me that apart from his army of werewolves, Kane also had a family. Eventually his wife, Cozbi, drank some of Kane's blood to gain the same ability as Kane had. She was a wicked woman who killed simply for sport and enjoyment. What forever cemented the hatred between Kane and Hayden was that Hayden slaughtered Cozbi and sent parts of her body to all the ends of the earth, so wherever Kane was hiding, he would be reminded of what Hayden did. Before her death, she and Kane had five children together: Antipas, Jehoram, Absalom, Juno, and Enoch. Hayden had had altercations with each of them numerous times, which resulted in the eventual deaths of Antipas and Jehoram. However, Absalom, Juno, and Enoch survived. Enoch was the youngest of the children. As well as being a wolf man, Enoch was also a shapeshifter who could even split into two different entities at once.

"Ouch, I'm sorry I asked."

"At least you know what we're up against now. After so many years, you can't blame me for doubting you."

"So I won your trust?" I asked.

"Let's just say you're working on it."

A horn sounded as he finished speaking. We both hurried over to the kitchen window and saw Bear's truck barreling down the driveway towards the house. It was a relief to see them and to know that they all were okay. I rushed out the door to greet them and Hayden slowly followed behind me. Bear came to a stop, and the gang all piled down from the monstrous truck.

"Connell ... you're okay," Lilly said, throwing her arms around me and planting a kiss on my cheek.

She made me think of Kevin, and my heart sank a little. I mustered a response. "I sure am."

She pulled away from me and held me at arm's length. "What's wrong?"

I smiled at her and lied, "I'm fine, really, I'm just happy to see you."

Bear walked right up to me and slapped me on the back with his giant, calloused hands. "Good to see ya, boy. I hope y'all made yourself at home?"

I shook his massive rough hand and said, "It feels like home."

Bear pushed on passed me, ran up to Hayden, and picked him up off the floor. "There you are, you old salty dog, I missed you," he screamed.

"Okay, Bear, it's good to see you too," Hayden said, motioning for Bear to put him down.

I watched as the three of them retreated into the house. It was such a good feeling to have them here. I just wished Doc and Toby had that same opportunity.

"Hey, stranger, how are you?" a soft voice asked behind me.

Swiftly turning around, I saw her. She was beautiful, and she had her hair up in pigtails with the pink on one side. "I'm better now that you're here," I said, reaching out and hugging her.

She squeezed me back tightly and started to cry. I held on to her for a few minutes and did not say a word.

"I thought you were dead," she murmured hysterically, squeezing me harder.

I pulled her away from me and held her by the hands. "Come on, you know it would take more than that to keep me away from you."

She chuckled, and I wiped her tears away. She slowly raised her eyes to meet mine. I could see so much feeling in those eyes that I got lost in the minute and kissed her. She hesitated at first, but she quickly drew me closer to her. We shared our first real kiss right there. It was full of passion, relief, and hope.

"I don't know what I would have done if I'd lost you," I whispered in her ear.

She pulled away from me, took me by the hand, and led me to the barn. Once we were there, we entered the tack room; she looked around for a second and made her way around to the other side of the saddles.

Leaning over them towards me she said, "This is where I first knew."

Puzzled, I looked around trying to figure out what she was talking about, but, after a few seconds, I had to admit I had no clue. "First knew about what?"

She smirked, grabbed me by the shirt, and pulled me towards her and the saddle. "This is where I first realized that I was in love with you."

She kissed me again; it was gentle and I could feel her taking over my spirit. I'd never felt anything like it before. This was a moment I wished I could freeze in time and live in forever. Just her and me without a care in the world. As she slowly backed away, our eyes met, and we shared a giggle.

"What now?" I asked.

"I don't know. How about we just enjoy today and worry about tomorrow when it gets here?" she replied.

I reached out and grabbed her hand. Leading her out of the barn, I looked back and said, "Deal."

We hurried over to the house and joined the group on the back porch. They were all gathered together, snacking on some of Bear's alligator jerky and their favorite sodas. Hayden tossed me another banana beer, and Andie Rae grabbed some type of grape concoction. We sat around telling stories about Doc and Toby with a tear being shed every now and again. It was the first time we had been able to grieve for our friends as a group. It felt like family, and I finally belonged and fit in. Heck, even Hayden was being nicer to me than normal.

We had been talking for hours, and the sun was starting to set when unexpectedly Hayden lifted his bottle and said, "To Doc and Toby, two of the finest warriors and brothers anyone could have the pleasure of knowing."

"To Doc and Toby," we all shouted, slamming our glasses together and taking a sip to commemorate our fallen comrades.

"I am so hungry I could eat the south end of a north-bound skunk," Bear proclaimed, looking through the pizza flyers.

"Bear, that is disgusting," Lilly shouted at him while we made our way indoors.

"Who peed in your Cheerios, Lilly?" Bear said.

"Do you always have to be so vulgar?" Andie Rae asked.

"Girls, the way I see it, if ya don't say what ya feel, your life is as useless as a pocket in your underwear," he said, dialing the number to order pizza.

"Hayden, do something with him, will you," Andie Rae shouted.

Shrugging his shoulders Hayden said, "If I knew how to fix him, I would have done it a long time ago."

While Bear finished up ordering the pizza, we gathered in the bonus room to talk about our next steps. It was clear from the girls that Tammy had not made any contact with the shop for weeks; however, Lilly did put eyes on her at Chamberlain. We were not certain whether she didn't have anything to report or if her disappearing act at the white house had raised some eyebrows. We agreed that, for her safety, we needed to leave her alone and allow things to cool down.

"The pizza will be here in about twenty minutes," Bear announced, entering the room.

"Thanks, Bear," said Hayden. "We're trying to figure out our next move. Grab a chair."

"Why don't we just go back to the white house and grab Enoch while we know their location?" I asked.

"They never stay at the same place once it's discovered," Lilly said.

Frustrated, Hayden snapped at me. "If it were that easy, we would have done it already, pansy."

Leaning back in my chair, I crossed my arms and shot back, "Seems like we're back to reality already."

Tilting forward, Andie Rae retorted, "Calm down, Hayden, he wouldn't know that."

He let out an enormous sigh and said, "Sorry, pansy." He explained that the werewolves moved around and bought new places as soon as one was discovered. Often, they would burn the old place down to cover their tracks, but it was very rare for them to sit idle too long. We were looking on the internet for possible places the next attack could occur, but we had to accept that our two best scouts were now gone.

The doorbell rang. Bear leaped up and hurried off to get the pizza. He returned after a few minutes and dropped the boxes and plates on the coffee table.

"Eat up, boys and girls," he said, right before taking a bite of a large slice of sausage, pepperoni, bacon, and ham.

Everyone took a slice or two and studied their phones or laptops for any clues as to the location of the next hit. As the night went on, it was clear that we were going to strike out this month and be on the sidelines, hoping nothing would happen. I could see the defeat on Hayden's face, but, at the same time, he was trying his best not to take it out on anyone. He scrolled like a madman through his phone.

Wiping her mouth, Lilly spoke up and asked, "When is the full moon next month?"

"December fifteenth," Hayden immediately answered without looking it up.

"Well, why don't we look to see what we can find on that night?" She took another bite of her pizza.

We agreed and started to thumb through upcoming calendars of events. With it being close to Christmas, there were hundreds of options to choose from. I felt like we were looking for a needle in a haystack when it hit me.

"What was that date again?" I asked.

"December fifteenth, why?" Hayden asked.

I leaped out of my chair and flipped rapidly through my phone. Pacing back and forth, my patience for Bear's lagging internet connection was starting to break. Finally, the page loaded, and I started to navigate throughout the site.

"Where is it?" I shouted.

"What? Where is what, pansy?"

I threw my hands up in the air, pumping my fists in victory while my phone sailed across the room and smacked against the far wall. "*Yes*—I knew it!" I screamed.

"What, Connell, what did you know?" Lilly inquired, standing up and pulling my arms down to get my attention.

"The winter bonfire.It's on December fifteenth at Chamberlain," I responded hysterically. "Don't you all see it? So many of them are attached to that school, it would be the perfect place to trap a bunch of people and make a quick meal out of them."

Taking another bite of pizza, Bear muttered with his mouth full of food, "Now you're digging where there's taters."

Looking at Bear with disapproval, Andie Rae stood up and made her way towards Hayden. "Well, what do you think?"

Hayden crossed his arms and looked down at the floor for a few minutes, deep in thought. My hope that he found my idea as brilliant as the rest of the group was fading with each tick of the clock. After a few more seconds, I threw my hands up in the air, and headed towards the kitchen to grab another drink. I pulled on the door in anger and the glass bottles rattled against themselves, snapping me out of my fit. I took a deep breath, opened another banana beer, took a quick swig, and returned to the group, who were all sitting again, looking defeated.

I plopped down on the sofa and asked, "So it appears you shot down my idea?"

"No, pansy. Stop being so negative," Hayden shot back quickly. "I think you're dead on, but here is the problem: the numbers." He grabbed a piece of paper that had some scribble on it and handed it to me. "I tried to estimate how many Enoch would have at that school, and, even with Toby and Doc, we would still be short."

I leaned back and studied the paper, taking in everything he'd said. It felt helpless—this game of cat and mouse had to end at some point. From our last encounter, it was apparent that they were thinking the same thing. If we were going to do this, we would have to go for the kill, pull out all the stops, and try to end it once and for all. I knew that was easier said than done, but the good thing was we didn't need scouts for this mission because I knew that school inside and out.

Time went by slowly, and we shared ideas here and there. It seemed like nothing was good enough to overcome the odds. The group was growing tired and frustrated, so Andie Rae went off to the kitchen and brought us back some milk and homemade cookies. I knew she'd always been the mother figure to the group, and, no matter how much Bear got on her nerves, she was aware how appreciative and how protective he was of her. Bear smiled and pulled the cookie apart. He allowed the melted chip to drip onto his tongue before inhaling the entire cookie in one swoop. I bent over and grabbed one myself. As I munched on it, I watched everyone enjoy the treat in their own special way. After all the ups and downs, the fights and tears, as well as the doubts I had of joining this crazy group, I felt at home and fit in with a group. While not everyone would agree or understand our intentions, we were put in the here and now for a purpose. At that moment, another group popped into my head. One that had a very similar to this band of misfits.

"*YES!*" I shouted, standing up. "I got it, you all have to trust me, but I think I got it."

Swigging down his last bit of soda, Bear stood up and headed towards the bathroom saying, "Boy, I tell you what, your brain is busier than a cat covering crap on a marble floor tonight."

"Bear, that is so gross," Lilly screamed, throwing a coach pillow at him.

"Don't mind him right now, Lilly," I said, smirking. "I'll go to Chamberlain tomorrow, and, from there, I'll be able to share my plan with you."

Hayden stood up, crossed his arms, and looked at me doubtfully. "Chamberlain? You want to put yourself in the line of fire again?"

"Hayden's right, Connell," Andie Rae asserted. "It's not safe for you there."

I walked over to both of them and put my hands on their shoulders. "Guys, you have to trust me, okay?"

They looked at each other for a moment. After a few seconds, Hayden knocked my arm off his shoulder and said, "Fine, but I hope you know what you're doing."

When Bear returned from the restroom, we cleaned up, and people started to head to bed. With Bear back in the house, I was exiled from his bedroom and had to make my way to the barn. Climbing up to the loft, I found nice setup. It was a fully enclosed room with a stereo, bed, bathroom, and two doors that swung open to expose the night sky.

I pushed up the doors as far as I could to see the stars and nearly full moon shining brightly to greet me. I leaned against the barn door for a few minutes and thought about all we'd been through and all that we'd lost. I was not sure if my plan was going to work, but something just told me this was the path we needed to go down. I sat down in the opening, let my feet hang, and started to talk to my folks as I often did. It would have been so wonderful to have them here for advice—it had been very hard since they died. Yeah, Grandma was here physically, but mentally, that cruel disease had taken her away as well. Until now, I'd felt all alone—that I always let people down, including myself. For the first time in a long time, I felt part of something, and I didn't want to lose that feeling.

Suddenly, the radio started to play "I Swear" by John Michael Montgomery. I swung around and found Andie Rae standing there with her phone plugged into the radio. I stood up, dusted my pants off, and smiled at her.

"Hi, I hope you don't mind company?" she asked, walking towards me.

"No, of course not," I said, going to close the barn doors.

"What are you doing that for?" she said, pushing them back open.

Perplexed, I rubbed a hand through my hair. "Because I remembered what you said about the sky and all."

She looked down, smiling. "I did say that, good to know you were listening." She looked out at the sky. "But I think I've lived in the past long enough. I need to start living for today."

She took me by the hand, and we both sat in the barn doors and let our feet dangle off the edge. We did not say anything for a while. She simply laid her head on my shoulder. We held each other's hands and stared at the stars, listening to her playlist.

"So, what do we do from here?" I asked.

"We do the best we can to live in the moment—that is all we are promised," she replied.

"It sure is beautiful tonight," I said, looking around again. "There's only one thing that could make it nicer."

Giggling, Andie Rae said, "Yeah, what's that?"

I turned towards her and leaned in slowly. "This."

I kissed her for a good while, and she kissed me back. I felt all the tension and anxiety that had built up in her for years, keeping her guard up, disappear. She was finally free to be herself and to love again. Maybe it was because she finally accepted that it was not her fault, or perhaps it was because she knew I was like Hayden and should be around a while. Whatever it was, that energy transferred to me in an electrifying way. After kissing for a few more minutes, her body started to relax. She put her arms around me and teared up. We leaned back and lay down on the wood floor, staring at the sky for hours before falling asleep in each other's arms.

Chapter 14
Purpose

The roosters were crowing, and the sun was just peeking over the horizon when I awoke in the barn with a sore back, all alone. Stretching with a massive yawn, I got up from the floor and bustled over to the bathroom to get ready for the day. Andie Rae, once again, had gotten up way before me and had time to lay out some clothes for me of her choosing. She'd set out some jeans and a long-sleeve, fitted red shirt. After dressing and doing a quick time check, I made my way out of the barn and into the kitchen of the house where I found the girls already eating breakfast.

Pouring some juice in a cup and placing it in front of me, Lilly asked, "Good morning, Connell. Did you sleep well?"

I hesitated for a second and looked past her, smiling. I could see Andie Rae frantically waving to let me know Lilly did not know about last night. "It was the best night I've had."

Andie Rae put her hand to her face and rocked while she tried to hide her smile. "Two or three eggs?" she asked.

"Two, please," I responded, holding out my plate as she dropped them on it. "Where's Hayden?"

Buttering her biscuit, Lilly said, "He had to run some errands, so he took off early."

"I'm going to assume Bear is still sleeping, right?"

Andie Rae put a large plate of bacon on the counter, and said, "Not for long."

I heard Bear scream from the hallway, "I'm so hungry my belly is rubbing a callous on my backbone."

He entered, give both the girls a kiss on their checks, and slapped me on the back so hard that my food shot out of my mouth. While I recovered from the massive blow, Bear grabbed the plate of bacon, some mayo, and an Italian loaf of bread, making himself a sandwich. I sat in amazement, globs of mayo dropping out with each bite, as he inhaled this monstrosity of a sandwich. I soon heard the cuckoo clock go off and checked the time. It was now seven in the morning, and I had about ninety minutes to get to Chamberlain.

After cleaning my mouth on my napkin, I took one last swig of my juice and asked, "What car should I take?"

Lilly pulled out some keys from her pocket and said, "Take the Dodge parked next to Bear's truck."

She tossed the keys over to me, and I snagged them out of the air. I hustled my way towards to the door yelling back, "Wish me luck—I'll see you all later."

I ran to the side of the house. They'd given me the keys to the most beat-up, rusted-out, and smelly car on earth. I opened the door and listened to it cry out in pain from not being oiled in decades. I jumped onto the long, vinyl bench front seat. Looking around, the first thing I noticed was that the car had an eight track and a push button radio for changing the channels. Shaking my head in disappointment, I found a sticky note on the seat expressing the hope I'd be safe and saying they didn't want me sticking out, hence this car and not one of their nicer ones. I turned the engine over, and it started right up and hummed, indicating the engine was well taken care of.

"So you may not look pretty, but apparently you have it where it counts," I said to the car as I drove off towards the highway.

I sped down the interstate, making my way in and out of traffic, and trying to get to Chamberlain in enough time to execute my plan. It seemed like the more I rushed, the longer it was taking me. I tried to calm down, and went through the plan again in my mind to distract myself. At last I found myself on Busch Boulevard, heading over towards Chamberlain. I was nervous and started to feel my stomach cramping.

"Calm down, Maxwell, it will be fine," I said, pulling into the circle since I did not have a parking pass.

There was a massive crowd near the Chief's Head gathering around the flagpole along with fire trucks and police cars flashing their lights. I quickly parked the car and ran over to see what was going on. When I approached the pole, I could not believe my eyes. It was Jack, and he looked like someone beat the snot out of him. He was tied to the flagpole, and he had a sign around his neck that simply read "This is what happens to bullies." The group of students around the scene were all from different hierarchies, each no doubt wondering who could have done this. It was not making much sense to me either.

I quietly maneuvered around the crowd, trying to eavesdrop on their conversations to see if anything they were saying made a lick of sense. The firemen were lowering Jack down, and he was looking a little worse than I was the day him and his lackeys got me in the locker room. With each movement, Jack moaned a little more until they placed him on the stretcher and took him away. As I walked past Dalton Fisk, our student body president, talking to a police officer, I could hear him describing the attacker.

"He had dark hair, scars on his face and arms, drove an old muscle car," Dalton said.

I was in shock—it was Hayden. He really took some interest in the beating I'd taken in the locker room and he'd left early today to run errands. "Well, what a surprise," I whispered.

"Did you hear him say anything?" the police office asked.

Dalton thought for a moment, and, after a few seconds, he snapped his fingers. "Yes, he walked up to the football team and asked which one was Jack, and when Jack answered, he tossed the others out of his way like they were flies and started to pound on him."

"Is there anything else he may have said or done?" the police officer probed.

Dalton signaled for the office to come closer and whispered, "Yes, sir, after he dragged Jack over to the flagpole and started to tie him to it, he growled like a large dog at the football team to stop them from attacking him from behind."

The office smirked and flipped his book closed. "Growled like a large dog?"

"Yes, sir."

The officer handed him his card, and, while he was walking away, he shouted back at Dalton, "Let me know if you remember anything else."

Dalton looked over the card and put it in his backpack before rejoining his friends to share the story once again. I was still taking it all in. I mean, there had been times when I didn't know who hated me more, Jack or Hayden. Looking back at the ambulance as it pulled out with its lights flashing, there was one thing I knew for sure at that moment; the outcasts were safe for at least the time being. With the crowd dispersing and people heading back to their normal hangout areas or to class, I quickly made my way over to the Chief's Head to find everyone debating amongst themselves about what had happened.

I waved and shouted at the gang. "Hey, guys, can you believe what happened?"

Xavier turned to see me, smiled, and waved back at me. "Well, look who it is. For a while, we weren't sure if you were ever going to show your face around here again."

Leaping out of her seat and throwing her arms around me, Greta added, "Connell, I missed you so much, this place is not the same without you."

Hugging her back, I asked, "Where're Santiago and Prisha?"

"You just missed them. They headed on to class already."

Xavier took a seat on the bench under the mighty Chief, leaned back, and put his arms behind his head. "So, are you going to tell us what you've been up to?"

Smiling at him, I said, "That's why I'm here. Remember, on the rooftop, you said you would have my back no matter what and to trust you?"

Xavier leaned forward, looking interested, and put his elbows on his knees. "Yeah, I do, why?"

"I'm here to cash in on that promise." Looking around to see who was nearby, I added, "But not here, we need to get the others and chat somewhere more private."

Suddenly, Ms. Whitehead's voice came over the loudspeaker. She dismissed school for the rest of the week while the police department continued its investigation. In addition, she asked that anyone who had any knowledge of the person who came on campus to attack Jack come forward and speak up.

Clapping my hands in enjoyment, I said, "This is our chance. Greta, go find the others and meet us back here."

She nodded. "Okay, but don't spill any gossip without me."

We watched her hurry off, and, when she turned the corner, Xavier reached over and pulled me closer to him. "Are you in trouble?"

I paused for a moment to take that thought in, put my arm on his shoulder, and said, "That, my friend, will be up to you."

Leaning back against the wall and crossing his arms, he retorted, "What does that even mean?"

"You'll see."

With the hoard of students pouring out of the school, the once-deserted area had become chaotic. Teachers were trying to get students who were waiting for the buses corralled; other students were driving themselves off campus. Looking around for the rest of the gang, I noticed that Mr. Farley was talking with Tammy, who was in tears. I didn't know if it was caused by what happened to Jack or by Mr. Farley. He did have a way about himself that brought out every emotion in a student. He took her by the arm and led her away back towards the office. His face was flushed, and I could tell he was annoyed about something.

Turning to Xavier, I asked, "Do you see Farley and Tammy?"

Looking out at the crowd, he spotted them and said, "Yes, and he doesn't look happy." Shaking his head, he continued, "I would not want to be Tammy right now."

I was silent for a moment and rubbed my chin before asking, "What do you think he would be mad at Tammy about?"

Shrugging his shoulders, Xavier answered, "No clue, but he's been chummy with Jack and his group lately."

"Why is that?"

Chuckling, Xavier said, "That's right, you haven't been here. Check this out, Mr. Farley volunteered to run the winter bonfire this year."

Perplexed, I said, "That's strange, the only thing he ever volunteers for is to punish people."

"He's been acting weird lately, like he was having an out-of-body experience."

"So he's being nice to everyone?"

"For the most part, but, like right now, he still has his moments where the real Mr. Farley stands up."

As I continued to ponder that, a thought popped in my mind that made total sense. What if Mr. Farley was Enoch? Jack and his group were all in on it, he was really nice to me after he saw my birthmark, and he did throw that piece of paper out that gave away the white house location. While I was still considering this theory, the rest of the gang showed up. After greeting both Prisha and Santiago, I signaled them to follow me over to the car, and we piled in. I decided to keep my idea to myself for now—I wanted to be certain before letting anyone else in on it. Sure, Farley had been a jerk in the past, but I did not want an innocent person to be our target. Pulling out of the visitors' lot, I sped away and made my way over to the local dive we all visited for our baked goods.

Looking up at the sign and realizing where we are, Prisha said, "Connell, you do know it's like nine in the morning, right?"

"Of course I do, but it's never too early for pie, right?"

"It's never too early for pie," Xavier proclaimed.

We jumped out of the car, hustled into the diner, and took a seat at the corner table. The waitress greeted us by name and asked Xavier if he wanted the usual; he confirmed he did. After taking the rest of our orders, she swiftly disappeared, only to reappear shortly with various types of pies, coffees, and milkshakes.

After a few bites in awkward silence, Santiago tossed down his spoon and asked, "*El pastel es Bueno, pero quiero saber que esta pasando.*"

Greta translated. "He said the pie is nice." She paused to take a sip of her iced coffee and continued, "But he wants to know what's going on, and so do I."

Sighing, I put my spoon down and crossed my arms on the table. "Okay, guys, I'm going to cut right to the chase with you all." I swallowed hard. "I need your help, and Chamberlain needs your help. I made a promise to myself a while back not to get you all involved, but I know now that's not possible if we are going to win."

"With what?" Xavier asked, then took another bite of his pie.

I looked around to make sure no one was near us and answered him in a whisper. "Fighting with werewolves."

Confused, Greta asked, "Like our role-playing game?"

I sighed and rubbed my face in frustration. "No. I'm trying to tell you guys that Chamberlain is going to be attacked, and it's up to us to stop it."

There was a stubborn silence for a moment and finally Santiago asked, "*¿Te golpeaste la cabezo o estas loco?*"

"He wants to know if you hit your head or if you're just crazy," Greta translated. "And so do I," she added curtly.

I rolled up my sleeve and showed them my birthmark. "Remember this? You all knew what it was, and you all had an idea what was happening around town, remember?"

"Yeah, but knowing about it is one thing, getting involved is another," Xavier answered.

Turning towards him I said, "Xavier, remember on the roof in Ybor when you said to trust you? Well, man, I am, and I'm asking for your help."

"Connell, we all have issues just getting off the bus and making it to the Chief's Head without getting bullied, beat up, or assaulted. How in the world do you think we have what it takes to save the entire school?" Prisha asked.

I put my hand over hers and answered, "Because I believe in you. I believe in us. I used to wonder who made the rules of our hierarchy, but now I understand why they existed. Perhaps they were there to prepare us for this very moment."

"So you're saying us getting our butts kicked daily was by design?" Greta asked.

"Maybe, but what I do know is if you all weren't picked on and bullied into the outcast group, you wouldn't have the knowledge that you do of the werewolves, and that will be key to our plan."

"But, Connell, it's just a game," Prisha countered.

"Is it?" Xavier asked. "I mean, we all knew for a while what was going on with these attacks, and we've read more about those creatures and practiced and studied the art of war every day for years." He looked each of them in the eye. "If not us, who?"

Everyone nodded in silence and Santiago said, "*Confiamos en que Connell, estamos a bordo.*"

"He said we all trust you and we're in," Greta said, smiling.

I closed my eyes for a second and did a quick fist pump with the team. We finished our food and started to chat about our next move. I simply told them there was a group of people I needed them to meet, and they had to trust me. Leaving the diner, I could sense they were all nervous and were not sure about what they had agreed to; however, I knew it was the right move. We, the outcasts, had been put here for a reason, and this was the reason. While we may not have been the strongest, best-looking, or most popular, we were loyal to each other, smart, and understood every aspect of the role-playing world. It was about time we used our strengths to turn the tables on the bullies and save our school, our town, and most likely our very lives. Driving off to Bear's, the only thing I still worried about was how Hayden would react to the new crop of troops I was bringing him.

Red Moon, White Moon

By Tom Cunningham

Chapter 15
Training Day

The car ride was long and silent. The tension was so thick that even with the air conditioner running at full blast, the cabin of the old Dodge was musty at best. As I pulled into the long driveway leading up to Bear's house, the group of outcasts who had become very special to me all looked around like little children going to the park for the first time. They really did not know what to expect, and they were eager to get a glimpse of where I was taking them. I parked the car next to Bear's truck, and we all piled out. I led them towards the house where the others were waiting on the porch.

"Come on, guys, it will be fine," I said, waving at Hayden and the others.

"I hope you're right, Connell. They don't seem too happy to see us," Xavier said.

I turned and smiled at him. "Actually, that is them in a good mood. Don't worry about it. It took me a while to get used to them, especially Hayden."

"Which one is Hayden?" Greta asked.

"The one with the dark hair and the scars on his face, eating the apple." I pointed.

Prisha grimaced and asked, "What happened to his face?"

"You'll understand in a minute." I whispered to myself, "I hope."

Tossing the half-eaten apple into the flowerbed, Hayden started to make his way towards us. "What is this, pansy?"

Looking back at my friends one more time with a smile to reassure them, I turned and answered, "They're what I went to Chamberlain for." I put my hand on Hayden's shoulder and said, "By the way, thank you for standing up to Jack for me, but I could have handled it."

He pushed my arm off his shoulder and walked past me. "I don't know what you're talking about, and we will leave it at that." He looked each of them up and down and asked them all, "Do you even know why he brought you out here?"

Xavier stepped forward. "Werewolf hunting."

Bear and the others who had joined us overheard Xavier and started to snort. "Y'all think ya have what it takes to kill some critters, do ya?" he asked.

Pointing at Bear, Santiago asked, "*¿Por que este hombre grande habla tan gracioso?*"

Bear, caught off guard, leaned in with his eyes wide open and asked, "Say what now?"

Greta rolled her eyes and quickly answered, "He was wondering why you talk funny." She turned to Hayden and said, "And you, please spare us the tough guy image—we get that all day, every day at Chamberlain. I'm here to help Connell, so either accept it or do not."

Hayden was speechless for a second. Then, he cracked a smile and extended a hand to her. "Okay, you got it. I am Hayden."

Greta smiled at him and shook his hand. "I'm Greta, nice to meet you."

After a few minutes of introductions, while I wondered why I didn't get the same treatment from Hayden in the beginning, we all went over to the barn where Hayden had been working on a plan based on what Lilly had told him about Chamberlain. Walking in, Xavier went right over to the map and started to look it over while we were still making small talk. He immediately grabbed a marker and his scenario book and started to make changes to what Hayden had already done, adding a few twists of his own.

"Son, perhaps you're as confused as a termite in a yo-yo right now, but I would stop mucking around with that board if I were you," Bear shouted from across the barn.

Hayden turned to see what Xavier was doing, marched over to him and took the marker out of his hand. "Pansy, I guess you have not explained to your friend how things work around here."

I quickly made my way between the two and said, "Calm down and let's hear him out—or do we want to waste time with this game some more?"

Hayden paused for a second, sighed and slapped the marker into my hand. "Fine, but it better be good."

I handed the marker back to Xavier and encouraged him. "Come on, Beast Slayer, this is what you're good at."

Xavier wiped the sweat off his brow, took the marker, and continued to change the plan around on the board. He pointed out simple fixes that would allow us to isolate the attack to the gym and football stadium. He had a few people positioned on the visitors' side to push the attack towards the gym. Others would be on the north side to make sure the monsters didn't escape to the tennis courts, and, finally, Hayden, Bear and I would be in the gym to pick them off one at a time as they entered.

"Makes perfect sense," I said, looking at everyone.

"Sure, it makes sense, but how do we know that y'all won't panic and run?" Lilly asked. "I mean, after all, you're afraid of some jocks and popular kids getting off the bus each morning."

"True, but unlike those scenarios, we've been training for this for years," Xavier said.

"Playing a game is one thing, looking those monsters in the eye and pulling that trigger is another," Andie Rae said.

Hayden finished the drink he'd been working on, tossed the empty bottle in a trash can, and stood up. "I guess there's only one way to find out."

Without warning, Hayden transformed into his wolf-man form, and all four of the newcomers scrambled away from his monstrous howl and sharp claws. He snatched up Xavier and pulled him close; Santiago picked up a chair and smacked it across Hayden's back. Dropping Xavier, Hayden turned his attention to Santiago, who slowly backed his way into a corner. Sensing how scared he was, I went to stand up and help him out, but Andie Rae reached out and pulled me back down into my seat. Greta and Prisha charged Hayden with some tools they found in the barn and swung them at his back and head. After a few blows, he turned his attention to the girls and ripped the tools out of their hands. Santiago used the opportunity to move out of the corner and regrouped with Xavier. They picked up some shiny pieces of sheet metal and blinded Hayden for a second, using the opportunity to grab a chain saw and hold it to his head. With the blade inches from his face, Hayden reverted to his human form and put his hand out to shake Xavier's.

I stood up, walked over, and took the chain saw out of Xavier's hand. "So why don't you fight back at school?"

Xavier, who was winded and very sweaty, answered, "Well, for a host of reasons."

"It's against the rules," Greta said.

"We're always outnumbered," Prisha said.

"Also, the pain associated with it," Xavier added. "We saw how bloody you were some days, and it just scared the heck out of us."

"And we weren't sure if the adults would believe us or actually help—it could just make the school year worse."

Lilly walked up to the four of them, shaking her head. "But you have no worries about fighting a wolf-man."

Wiping his brow with his sleeve, Xavier said, "It just seems different. There are no rules to break, it's right against wrong."

"*Ademas sabiamos que no iba a matarnos,*" Santiago added, crossing his arms and leaning against the wall.

Nodding in agreement, Greta decoded: "We all knew he wasn't going to kill us either."

Bear belched after finishing his fifth can of soda and said, "I'm telling y'all, when it's go time, y'all will be as anxious as a one-eyed cat watch'n two rat holes."

Xavier shook his head. "What now?"

Crossing her arms and looking disgusted by the belch, Andie Rae translated. "When it comes time to bring the fight, you will be anxious, scared, and a million other things."

I looked over at Hayden, who was grabbing some ice for the knot on his head. "So what do you think?"

Plopping down on the coach with the ice pack on his head, he said, "They need a lot of work, but they'll do."

We spent the next month following the same routine. Lilly would pick the four of them up at school and drive them to Bear's. We would practice our plan and eat together, followed by Andie Rae taking everyone home. Every now and then, Prisha would have to skip to work at her family's restaurant, which everyone understood. The last thing we wanted was to draw attention to ourselves. Each day would be smoother than the last, and we remembered more and more of our plan; we were able to act it out on instinct instead of reading it over and over to each other.

The full moon that month came and went. It was as red as ever, and as we ate our dinner on the back deck, staring at the moon, all types of emotions surfaced: anger, fear, sadness, disgust, and anticipation. It would soon be time for us to take action, and, to be honest, I was not sure how confident I was in the new members of our crew. After all, we had not worked in a unit during a full moon, and the last thing we needed was for half of our team to falter or panic. They showed well with Hayden, but they knew he wasn't going to kill them. It worried me how they would react when they saw all the blood, dead bodies, and actual werewolves who wanted nothing more than to tear them apart. If they fled for any reason, our plan could go south quickly, putting the team at risk.

It was the day before we were to face off with our enemies, and the team was mentally exhausted from all the prep work we had done over the last month. When the others arrived from school, they piled out as normal, getting ready to go through our routine. As they approached the house, Hayden came outside and signaled for us to join him inside.

Looking at me for some type of clue, Xavier asked, "What's this about?"

I smiled at him and answered, "I guess you're just going to have to find out for yourself."

"As long as it doesn't include more push-ups. I'm good with a change of pace," Greta said, walking past us.

We entered the house, and there was a huge meal prepared with all the fixings anyone could ask for. We all took a seat around the table, and Bear gave thanks for the team and our newsiest members. Shortly after, we started to dig into the meal, laughing and smiling at each other. Except Hayden, that was. I sat next to him, and he simply tilted his banana beer my way before taking a swig. We veterans knew this was the big one. This was our chance to finally eliminate Enoch and his machine of fury. If we failed, I did not think we would be planning a next time. We were all in, and, based on our last encounter, I felt we were changed to the point where we needed to celebrate with each other because we didn't know if it would be our last time.

Hayden stood up, tapped a glass, and lifted his drink to us. "I would like to make a toast. To Toby, Doc, and all the others who have given their lives to save ours. May our actions tomorrow justify the sacrifice they have made already."

We cheered for our lost friends, most whom I never knew, but I understood how brave they were. I just hoped I'd made the right decision by asking my new friends to join our crew. I hoped they understood what I saw in them and our kind—the outcasts. We spent the rest of the afternoon and evening enjoying each other, and everyone tried to block out tomorrow. Even Hayden chatted with Bear and Xavier. After sitting by myself for a few minutes more, I decided to stop worrying about what I could not control and just enjoy what I could; after all, I was in the presence of the finest outcasts I ever knew.

Chapter 16
The Veil Falls

It was the day of the winter bonfire, and we were as busy as ever preparing for that night. The four newest additions to the group were at school, as planned, to ensure that they were up to date on the plans for this evening and to make sure nothing had changed. Hayden had been nervous all morning because he hadn't been able to get hold of Tammy to give her a heads up. Although she was a werewolf, she had been so helpful to the team that we felt we owed her all the help we could give her.

Without Toby and Doc, we also felt the pressure to pick up the load and ensure we had enough gear for all nine of us. Bear, who was always in a good mood, whistled away as he snacked on some jerky. Andie Rae was trying to calm Hayden down as always, and Lilly was packing Doc's supply bag. She'd picked up that critical role and used the same bag Doc did. We tried to talk her out of it—it had bloodstains all over it—but she was having none of it.

The day was flying by, and before I knew it, Lilly slipped out the door and was on her way to go pick up the others. So many thoughts went through my mind at that moment: should I have gotten them involved, would any of them back out, and—most importantly—would they freeze when it was "go time." While I couldn't blame them if they did, we really couldn't afford it. The following hour was total anguish for me. I kept my eye on the driveway and jumped at every sound I heard to see if it was them pulling up.

Bear walked over to me and slapped me on the back. "Calm down, son. Worry is as useless as dried spit—if they come, they come."

Rubbing my back from where his massive hand made contact, I replied, "I know you're right, but so much is riding on tonight."

Taking another bite of jerky, he mumbled, "True, but you don't have control over that—now have some jerky."

"Thanks." I picked a piece of jerky off the plate that was inches from my face.

Andie Rae, who had joined us, picked up a couple of pieces and took a seat next to me. "Even if they back out, we have a solid plan."

"Yeah, I know, but I feel like we always play a cat and mouse game with them."

"What do you mean?" Andie Rae asked.

I stood up and started to pace. "I mean, we kill them, and they retreat. They kill some of us, and we retreat." I looked at the two of them, punched my left hand with my balled-up right one, and added, "I just want to finish them off."

"Calm down, pansy," Hayden said, walking into the barn. "You'll get your chance soon enough."

Andie Rae turned to Hayden, took the plate of jerky out of Bear's hand, and offered him some. "He's worried the group will back out, leaving us shorthanded."

Taking a piece of jerky, Hayden looked over at me and grinned. "Seems like you've come a long way from the first night in Ybor."

I chuckled, took a seat, and simply said, "Yeah, I have."

Soon after, I heard a horn in the distance and took off running towards the driveway. It was Lilly and the rest of the gang. I was so relieved to see that all four of them kept their promise. I greeted each one of them with a hug and put my arm around Lilly's shoulder as we made our way back to the team in the barn. Once there, we all sat around the map, and Hayden reviewed it one more time with us.

Looking at his watch, Hayden announced, "We have about two hours before we move out. Make sure you're ready to go."

Bear clapped his hands together and rubbed them vigorously. "I'm as nervous as a tick on dip day."

Hayden put his arm around Bear's shoulders and looked around the room. "Remember, if we stick to the plan, we'll be okay."

We nodded in agreement and began to prepare for the night's activities. Andie Rae briefed the four newest members of our clan on how to prepare for tonight and reviewed the guns they would be carrying one last time. They were all nervous, and Xavier had to wipe his forehead with his shirt. Lilly had her earphones in and was in the zone, listening to her music. Bear and Hayden, as normal, were off in the corner, chatting and enjoying a drink. I decided to check on the guys and make sure they were ready.

"Hey," I said to Xavier, walking over to him. "You all okay?"

Still sweating, he wiped his brow again and answered, "As good as we're going to be, I guess."

Looking around the room to make sure no one could hear me, I leaned in and whispered, "You know you don't have to do this, right?"

Xavier smiled and responded, "I told you I would be there for you, and I meant it."

I slapped him on the shoulder and said, "Thanks, man, it means a lot."

After checking with the other three and receiving similar responses, I started to prepare my gear as well. The next few hours flew by with everyone hustling around, finishing up their final prep work and going over the plan a few more times. With the time finally upon us, we gathered into our circle one more time and were led in prayer for our safety by Bear. As always, Hayden stayed away and stared at the mapped-out plan one last time.

When Bear finished, Hayden turned to us and said, "We're ready to go. Remember, stick to the plan, and you will be okay."

Picking up a clipboard from the desk, Andie Rae started to read off our car assignments. "Bear, you're with Hayden and

Connell. Lilly, you have Santiago and Greta. The others are with me."

Bear picked up his favorite shotgun and put it in his holster behind his back. "Last chance, boys and girls, if you feel y'all can't hunt with the big dogs, y'all should stay here on the porch," he screamed.

Without any objections, we all left the barn and piled into our assigned cars. Like always, Bear started to blast his radio as we tore down the driveway heading towards Chamberlain. The ride felt like it was faster than normal even though no one said a word the entire way there. Driving down Busch Boulevard, we could see the football stadium with its lights on and people starting to assemble in the stands. It was roughly thirty minutes before sundown, so we had to hurry to make sure we were in place in time. While the others parked in the student parking lot, we swung behind the school and parked on a side road. We hustled to the fence, jumped it, and snuck around to the back entrance of the gym. We waited until ten minutes before sundown before opening the gym and entering it. The place was dark, but we could hear moaning nearby.

Hayden looked at Bear and me and whispered, "Spread out and try to find out what that moaning is about."

We split up, and I went directly to the gymnasium's main floor while Bear checked out the bathrooms and Hayden entered into the locker rooms. The moaning was growing louder as I moved forward. I could see a person in the shadows, hanging from something, so I quickly looked for the lights and turned them on.

"*Tammy*!" I screamed, rushing over to her.

She was tied to a rope by her hands and dangling in the air. Her face was bloody, and she had a ton of claw marks all over her body. I tried wiping the blood off her face, but with each wipe, more blood gushed out of her wounds to take its place.

I lifted her face and asked, "Who did this to you?"

She mumbled a response, but I couldn't make out what she was saying because of the blood dripping out of her mouth.

"Guys, in here," I yelled.

Bear and Hayden ran into the gym and, seeing Tammy hanging there, rushed over to join us. "What happened, Tammy, talk to me," Hayden said, cutting her down with one of his claws.

She collapsed onto the floor, and Hayden scooped her up into his arms. We heard the gym doors open from behind us, and Bear and I spun around to find Mr. Farley and Mrs. Perry approaching us.

"Mr. Maxwell, what is going on here, young man?" he snarled.

Exposing Tammy's bloody body to them, I snapped back, "Why don't you tell me, you monster?" I pulled out my gun. "Ms. Perry, you need to get out of here now!"

Mr. Farley put his arm out and turned beet red. "I don't know what you're thinking, but you need to put that gun down, Mr. Maxwell. Now!"

"No, I know it's you," I screamed at him, "the way you treated me after you saw my birthmark, the note you threw in the trashcan, and you were the last one I saw with Tammy, yelling at her. Did you know she was feeding us information all along, you bastard?"

With his hands raised, he slowly walked towards me, once again asking me to be reasonable and place the gun down. Mrs. Perry followed behind him, not saying a word.

"Mrs. Perry, what are you doing? Get away from him, he's a monster," I pleaded.

Suddenly, Mr. Farley's body went stiff and convulsed for a second before dropping to the floor in a pool of his own blood.

Mrs. Perry, whose hand was now a bloody claw, snarled at us. "I thought he would never shut up."

Confused, I looked down at Mr. Farley's body and up at Mrs. Perry. "Wait, you are—"

"Enoch?" She cackled. "Yes, of course I am. Don't tell me you thought this idiot could pull off such a masterful plan."

Stopping to think about for a second, it made perfect sense. She talked to Farley the day I got beat up. She demanded to know about Bear and his crew. She was hanging out with Jack and the other werewolves. How could I have been so stupid?

Before I could say another word, Hayden laid Tammy down on the floor gently, stood up, and faced Enoch. "There is no escape for you tonight, Enoch."

"Hayden, how nice to see you again." With a devilish smile, she continued. "Why would I try to escape, since everything is going according to plan? Even your little spy couldn't stop me."

"We'll see about that," Hayden said.

"Boys, stick to the plan no matter what," Hayden said before rushing Enoch and changing into his wolf-man form.

"I've been waiting for this for a long time," Enoch snarled, changing into her wolf form.

The collision between the two sounded like a stick of dynamite igniting as they thrashed back and forth at each other. We didn't know if Tammy was still alive, but Bear picked her up and locked her in a supply closet in the hope that she was. Like clockwork, we heard the first rally of gunfire, screaming, and animated howls. Before Bear or I could react, the gym started filling up with werewolves being driven in this direction by the others. We picked them off as they entered. Behind us, Hayden and Enoch were locked in an intense battle, biting and clawing at each other. Blood was splattering everywhere, and we heard painful screeches every few minutes or so.

Bear signaled me to follow him out to the stadium, and, as we reached the door, I turned and saw Enoch slamming Hayden against the bleachers, knocking him unconscious. Enoch slowly circled around Hayden for the kill, and my instincts took over. I charged Enoch, screaming and feeling my birthmark burning. I lost all feeling and could see only in black and white. My sense of smell intensified, and I felt my body strengthen beyond comprehension.

Bear paused and shouted at me, "Hit that bastard so hard, she'll cough up bones!"

I slammed into Enoch, knocking her off Hayden and onto the floor. She stood up and sized me up and down. For the first time, I was in my wolf-man form. My claws were massive, and my fur was white as snow. Enoch snarled at me and charged. We bit, clawed, and pummeled each other viciously. With each strike, I grew stronger and could feel her growing weaker. I threw her into the visitors' bleachers, and she fell to her knees, a bloody mess.

I slowly made my way over to her beaten body and grabbed a hold of her jaw. She struggled with what little strength she had left, but she was no match. I pulled as hard as I could, and almost immediately, I could hear the sounds of bone cracking. She put up as much fight as she could, but with one last mighty pull, Enoch's jaw was snapped apart. She collapsed to the ground, lifeless. I put my arms over her chest and let out a monstrous howl of victory.

I hurried over to Hayden, transforming back to my human form somehow, and found that he had done the same thing.

I leaned over him and helped him to his feet, asking, "Are you okay?"

He was holding his hand over a bad gash on his chest. "Yeah, but she got the best of me." He looked past me to see her lifeless body lying in a pool of blood. "But it seems like I couldn't say the same about you."

We walked over to Enoch, and Hayden kicked her onto her back to examine the body. "Snapped jaw, I see."

Rubbing my head, I said, "Yeah, I guess you can say it's my thing."

"Nice work," he said.

Hayden made his way over and unlocked the door where Tammy was to check on her.

"She is gone," he said, bowing his head.

I leaned over Mr. Farley's body. He had a blank stare on his face, and his skin had started to turn white already. I wept.

"Mr. Farley, I'm sorry, you were a good guy after all," I said, closing his eyes.

The others came rushing into the gym, covered in blood. I made a quick spot check and saw Andie Rae and Lilly first. The others brought up the rear, but Prisha was missing.

"Prisha?" I asked the group, running up to them.

Xavier lowered his head and answered softly, "No."

Greta was consoling Santiago, who was crying for the loss of our friend, with tears pouring out of her eyes as well.

Xavier walked over to Enoch's body and asked, "So who was the mastermind?"

"Mrs. Perry," I answered.

"You got to be kidding me," he said.

"Yeah, I know. I thought for sure it was Farley," I said.

"Hayden," Bear said softly.

We all gathered around the closet where Hayden was kneeling with Tammy's head in his lap. He was stroking her hair softly, and he did something that shocked me: he cried.

Andie Rae approached me and hugged me. "We did it."

Hugging her tightly back, I answered, "Yeah, we did."

Hearing sirens, Lilly rushed over to the gym doors, opened them and shouted at us, "Come on, we got to get out of here."

Everyone piled out of the gym. Hayden gently placed Tammy's head on the floor, leaned over, and gave her a soft kiss. Standing up, he signaled for me and Bear to follow him out towards the stadium. As we walked out back towards the truck, we saw numerous monsters and students lifeless, drenched in blood while others were sobbing and being hugged by teachers. I saw Jack and his group in the distance, and they spotted us as well. Knowing their powers were gone, they ran out of sight, afraid of what we might do to them.

Looking back at Hayden, I asked, "What happens now?"

"For the ones who survived, their curse is broken now that Enoch is dead. This town can finally start to heal, and we are one step closer to Kane."

We jumped the fence and got into Bear's truck, speeding away into the night to meet up back at the house.

The next morning, I left the house early and headed back to the white house in Plant City. It was just like they said it would be: abandoned. Standing in the room where I'd confronted Kevin, all that was left were scribblings on the wall and some papers on the desk. I made my way out of the house and started back towards Tampa, wondering where he was.

I drove to Chamberlain; there were reporters, police, and yellow tape everywhere. The mighty werewolf chief was gone, and I just stood there taking it all in. The others pulled up shortly after and came over to me.

"I thought you might come here," Andie Rae said, hugging me.

Hayden handed me the paper and said, "Seems like school is closed until further notice."

I read the headline: "Massacre at Chamberlain High." The story covered the wild dog attack and how the town was under curfew at night until they could determine that the threat was gone.

"What happens now?" I asked.

"Well, if I know Kane, he will be sending the Twins to deal with this," Hayden said.

"The Twins?" Lilly asked.

"Yeah," said Hayden. "Enoch's older siblings. Much more dangerous."

"What's our play, you old salty dog?" Bear asked.

Hayden smiled. "Go at them with everything we have."

Bear slapped him on the back in approval, and everyone got into their vehicles to head over to the shop.

"You coming?" Andie Rae asked.

"Yeah, I'll be along in a minute," I answered.

"Don't take too long," she said, kissing me before heading over to Lilly and the others.

I had an uneasy feeling about what the future held for us. We'd lost so much already, and we were only dealing with one werewolf chief; now, it was going to be twins. At that moment, I knew I was done with school and was now a full-fledged member of the asylum. I felt guilty about what had happened to Prisha, Mel, Kevin, and Tammy. I remembered at the beginning of the year I'd wanted Jack and his pride of pukes to pay for what they did to my kind, but now that they had, some with their lives, I didn't feel like I thought I would.

I finally understood what it meant to be an outcast. We were a special breed put here to achieve great things. Some would be bankers, dentists, doctors, or engineers to make the world better place. For me, it meant I was going to rid the world of evil people like Jack and his clan. In the end, bullies only have the power we allow them to have. We don't always have to resort to violence to stop them. Sometimes, we just come together and say enough is enough. I got into my car and headed back to the shop, leaving my old life behind me at the Chief's Head. I was looking forward to seeing what destiny had in store for me.

Red Moon, White Moon

By Tom Cunningham

Made in the USA
Lexington, KY
03 February 2019